Marianne Kendall has always scribbled, but any serious attempt at writing was pushed aside by the more urgent demands of life. She had a varied career but, at thirty years old, with no marriage, no job and two small children, she decided to become an accountant. It paid the bills. It was later in life that she fell into lecturing, publishing a book on international finance. She now lives quietly, cooking, entertaining friends, and annoying her children.

Marianne Kendall

FAMILY MATTERS

AUSTIN MACAULEY PUBLISHERS™

LONDON • CAMBRIDGE • NEW YORK • SHARJAH

A CIP catalogue record for this title is available from the British Library.

ISBN 9781398423220 (Paperback)
ISBN 9781398423237 (ePub e-book)

www.austinmacauley.com

First Published 2022
Austin Macauley Publishers Ltd®
1 Canada Square
Canary Wharf
London
E14 5AA

Chapter 1

"Damn!" She fingered the bright pink area carefully.

"This sucks! It's getting bigger!" After all, this was important, like choosing the right heel height and bewailing the plight of neglected donkeys in hot and horrid Mediterranean countries. Let alone persuading house buyers that they were in no immediate danger of contracting chickenpox, or any other kind of pox. Where was the benefit of restricting one's chocolate intake if this was the result?

Kimberley sat back from examining her chin in the rear-view mirror, squirming a little, as she felt the warm, clammy leather through her silk blouse. Rain was on the way and the air was as thick as treacle. She returned her attention to the job in hand. Noting the time so she wouldn't exceed the free hour that Ronaldsway airport allowed, she got out of the car and made her way to the Arrivals area, fervently hoping that Bob's plane wouldn't be late. An extended wait on a soggy Wednesday evening in September did not appeal, and back at the house her step-mother Irene would regard it as a near-catastrophic disruption to the household arrangements. Irene steadfastly ascribed all unpleasantness and inconvenience entirely and exclusively to the person she considered at fault; airline delays were no exception. This knowledge of a possible frosty reception was combined with Kimberley's own irritation at having to leave work early. A house viewing – one that promised to be very profitable – had to be handed over to that smarmy little moron she worked with.

However, she was pleased to have the opportunity to talk with her brother alone on the journey back home. She could prime him about the family company's deteriorating financial position as well as find out what was going on in London. She knew that the reason he gave Irene for flying back home early – to have a chance to study the latest monthly accounts – was just not true. Bob never studied anything if he thought he could get away with it. His quick mind could analyse figures immediately. Too bad the last few months' were so awful.

A rather tired announcement warning travellers not to leave their luggage unattended brought her attention back to the present. Some passengers started to come through from the baggage hall. Kimberley spotted Bob coming towards her. He was walking over to her as perky as you please and talking with a great deal of animation with a guy walking alongside him. The contrast between them was striking. Bob looked the typical undergraduate with his fresh complexion, long, untidy hair and an eager friendliness radiating from eyes as blue as the motorway signs. With an easy smile, he acknowledged his sister. Then he turned to continue talking with his companion. But, the other man… He was another pair of shoes altogether. Sort of Christian Slater meets Novak Djokovic. This merited some attention.

He was plainly not one of Bob's university friends – he had at least another decade's worth of dignity. He was wearing a suit under a very well-tailored raincoat, which suggested a business purpose. Who wears a suit flying to a holiday destination? And there was something foreign about his looks; a dusky, golden skin tone, intensely black hair and intelligent eyes of the same colour, a straight, strong nose and a generous but compressed mouth. Mediterranean possibly, or even further east; Turkish? Arab? Or even Romany? Whatever his origin, not only Kimberley's but several other passengers' gaze lingered on him more than was polite as he strode across the concourse. His whole demeanour showed confidence and resolution yet with a certain lack of pretentiousness. But his expression implied a preoccupation with something he did not especially care for even though he seemed amenable to his young escort's chatter. Juggling with various pieces of luggage threatening to overflow the airport trolley, he drew out a mobile phone and began to dial, looking rather crossly around him. Who on earth had Bob picked up now?

"Hi, Kim! Paul, meet my favourite sister. Kimberley, this is Paul – Paul Panesar."

"That's plausible," thought Kimberley. *"I can't imagine him as a Wayne."*

But Mr Panesar was still engaged with his call and gave the appearance of counting up to ten as he berated the hapless person on the other end.

The surname certainly sounded foreign. "What's going on?" muttered Kimberley as Bob handed her first his small holdall then, from the trolley, those of the irate traveller. Her earlier irritation had by now been replaced by a puzzled frustration at this unexpected development. And now Bob was trying to usher him out of the terminal towards the car park.

"It's okay to give Paul a lift, isn't it, Kim?"

"Sure. Hello! Nice to meet you," she said brightly and extended her hand, but her smile faded as the new acquaintance merely nodded and, tight-lipped, pocketed his phone. *"Suit yourself,"* she thought, considerably offended. His manner suggested he might as well have arrived during an Arctic winter rather than a warm, humid evening on the Isle of Man. To Bob she remonstrated, "It's very late. We ought to go straight home. Irene wants to talk with you before she goes to bed. Trust me, there are a lot of things to discuss. Have you read the reports?"

On a scale of one to ten, Bob's interest in what she was saying reached about, oh, one and a half. As they entered the car parking area, Kimberley tried once more to start a conversation, reluctant to give up on the alluring but brusque stranger. "Did you fly here together?"

"Yes," interjected Bob. "I bought the last copy of 'The Economist' at the Airport, but he refused to let me sell it on to him – at a humungous profit, of course. Then we found ourselves sitting across the aisle from each other on the plane so I very generously lent it to him to read and we got chatting. Paul's not been to the Isle of Man before so I thought we'd show him how friendly the natives are. And I knew you wouldn't mind giving him a lift on this lovely evening – well, it would be if it weren't starting to pour with rain. It looks as if his taxi hasn't turned up. Should have organised a hire car from us, shouldn't he?"

Kimberley merely smiled while Bob extolled to his new friend the benefits of dealing with a reliable local company. On reaching the car, he opened the rear door and was busy trying to cram his reluctant companion and accompanying luggage into it while Kimberley got in and started the engine.

"It's not the natives that have a problem about being friendly," thought Kimberley. *"Trying to start a conversation with him is like trying to light wet paper,"* but she had noticed that Mr Panesar – Paul – had begun to smile slightly, while Bob recounted how they had met. *"That's better,"* she said to herself, *"you should try that more often."* Aloud she said, "Where do you want to go?"

"Look, I'm sorry. It's late, and you're obviously in a hurry. I let myself be persuaded by your brother to accept a lift, but it's quite all right – I'm sure I can easily get a taxi back in the terminal."

He was disengaging himself from the car and Bob's efforts when Kimberley abruptly let out the clutch, throwing him back in the seat. "It's no trouble," she lied, hoping the insincerity did not reach her voice. "Let's prove just how friendly we natives are. Where to?"

"Thank you," he muttered, recovering his breath with his composure. "Moncrieff Hotel. It's somewhere on the promenade in Douglas. I need to find out what's gone wrong. I hope they will still have a reservation for me."

She moved off as quickly as the traffic would allow but the rain had now started to come down steadily, and every vehicle seemed intent on moving unnecessarily slowly out of the airport car park. (*"We're gonna get mildew at this rate,"* observed Bob.) She was now getting annoyed about agreeing to the lift but the hotel was not far out of their way, so she tried to persuade herself that it would not delay their arrival home by much. "Do you want to drive?" she asked Bob, sensing his impatience also.

"No. Can't," then added in answer to her startled glance, "lost my licence last week."

"So that's why you flew! What happened?"

"Nothing much. It was just bad luck. I'll tell you later. But don't say anything to Mum, will you? I don't want to upset her at the moment. Let's change the subject. Hey, Paul, if you do want to hire a car from us – the name's Weatherby's and we're not far from your hotel. I can guarantee you a very substantial discount. We specialise in top-of-the-range models, and very nice they are too. Do you have a favourite car in mind?"

Their passenger shrugged. "No." And he clearly didn't care.

"And then you could use it to come to the firm's annual summer barbecue next Sunday," persisted Bob. "I have one of my big surprises planned!"

If a flicker of distaste flashed across his face, only Kimberley noticed it. Or maybe it was a trick of the passing lights. She felt uncomfortable with Bob chatting so freely about the family business. Not that she was directly involved. She had long ago decided she preferred property to petrol and started a career in estate agency. Besides, she was frequently at odds with Irene. They seldom actually fell out, but both recognised an underlying tension mixed with mutual respect. Seeing less of each other removed any latent friction. Nevertheless, she had some sympathy with her stepmother, knowing Irene would have a fit if she heard her son promising cut-price deals and issuing barbecue invitations to events meant strictly for employees and their families. Discounting was one of the issues she knew would be raised in Friday's board meeting.

Paul was now smiling faintly in a rather embarrassed fashion at the invitation, and Kimberley's worthy compulsion to enforce harmony rushed in to defend him from Bob's enthusiasm. "Maybe Mr – er – Paul doesn't want to hire a car, let alone come to a silly corporate event. Taxis could suit him better unless he's planning to do a lot of driving. It depends on what he's planning. How long will you be staying?"

"That depends on many things," came the uninformative reply.

Kimberley went back to concentrating on her driving and the conversation petered out except for Bob describing the island's charms. Occasionally she glanced back in the mirror to check her initial impression of the unappealing Mr Panesar. There was no question that he was remarkably good-looking with his striking dark colouring and unshakable self-possession. He had undone his suit jacket and, despite some unspoken tension hovering about in the car, he nevertheless appeared very relaxed, peering out of the window from time to time at objects still visible in the deepening evening gloom.

Bob's narrative failed as they approached the Fairy Bridge at Santon, and he gave a sly sideways smile at his sister. In unison, they raised their hands in salute and solemnly murmured, "Good evening, Little People."

In the mirror, Kimberley saw an abrupt, bewildered frown cross their passenger's face.

Bob turned in mock alarm. "Quick, quick, say 'Good evening!'" There was a disbelieving silence from the rear seat. "Don't say I didn't warn you. You'll have bad luck now – even more."

"Why do you say that?"

Bob explained the Manx custom of appeasing the many supernatural inhabitants of the island. But Mr Panesar was egregiously unimpressed.

"You don't believe that nonsense, do you? Surely no one does."

Kimberley was riled at the supercilious tone of the newcomer. Folly or not, you did not ridicule local beliefs and routines. "On the island, many people still take it very seriously. Even the TT riders come to this bridge to guarantee their luck in the races. Several did a couple of weeks ago when some races were on." And he won't make many friends here with an attitude like that, she thought but kept that opinion to herself.

"And there are lots more – the Buggane, the Moddhey Dhoo and the Phynodderee," added Bob. But there was no response from behind. He evidently was not straining his attention to absorb Bob's information. The conversation ceased.

Bob wriggled in his seat, irritated that his conversational skills were not being utilised.

"Kim, why has the meeting been moved to Friday at the last minute?"

"Sir Philip Galbraith died a week ago last Sunday, and Irene wants to go to the funeral, which is tomorrow."

Their passenger leant forward with sudden interest. "Do your families know each other?" he asked in an intense voice.

Bob obligingly started to fill in the details. "Yes. Our father was Sir Philip's business partner, long before he became a 'Sir'. Although he was a lot older than Dad, they co-founded a software company, Braithby Business Solutions."

Kimberley felt obliged to intervene to prevent Bob from saying more than was appropriate. "As the business grew, they differed on several matters so agreed to part. Sir Philip bought Dad out very generously, and Dad started the car dealership with the proceeds."

"With the little money that was left after Mum insisted he bought Prospect Hall," said Bob sounding uncharacteristically judgmental.

"Bob, I'm sure Paul isn't interested in our family affairs. He must be tired and just wanting to reach his hotel. Give it a rest."

Silence reigned again as the journey progressed. When they arrived at the hotel Bob helped Paul out with his luggage. They exchanged a few words – no doubt Bob was once more urging him to hire a car – then the brother and sister set off home.

"Nice guy."

"As charming as a pedal bin as far as I'm concerned. I like people but they have to be more than just alive and breathing. He must have been a pallbearer in a previous life. The only time he showed any interest in anything was when he asked about our family's involvement with Sir Philip. Obviously, a social climber, certainly not worth being late for. I hope I never see him again." Though Kimberley would have been mighty unhappy if she knew how futile her wish would prove to be. "Why on earth did you offer him a lift? You know Irene goes ape when anyone upsets her routine. Think of the rest of us. There are enough problems with the business at the moment without you making this evening more acrimonious than it needs to be."

"Easy, Tiger! I'll sweet-talk Mum when I get there. Don't worry; she won't blame you if that's what you're worried about. Anyway, what's likely to be the main problem at Friday's meeting? I left my accounts package at the flat."

Kimberley groaned at his carelessness. "Both new and used sales are still falling, no one's been hiring throughout the summer, and overheads are going through the roof. Even allowing for the general slowdown in business, things are bad. Being so dependent on the inflated salaries in the financial services sector leaves us very exposed at the moment. We're not going to solve the problem by cutting back on paperclips. And the talks about the new distributorship with the Indian company aren't going well. Let's wait and see what the others have to say on Friday. There's not much point in discussing things in more detail if you haven't looked at the figures. In the meantime, how did you lose your licence?"

"I smashed my car up again a few weeks ago – it's a write-off this time. I was breathalysed and," he grinned across at her sheepishly, "I was more than three times over the limit. The police threw the book at me. I was done for speeding, dangerous driving, criminal damage to police property, abusive behaviour, the lot. I admit I was doing over the ton but it was on the M1 late at night when it was deserted, hardly anyone else around. I was perfectly safe. Anyway, this car was sitting on my tail so I thought we'd have a bit of a race. After about a mile, it overtook me – and switched on a blue flashing light! I was so cross with myself that I braked a bit too hard and there must have been some oil or gravel on the road. The car slewed round and smashed into the back of the police car, bounced off a bridge support and turned over. But," he sighed with relief, "I had my seatbelt on so at least I didn't get done for that, this time!"

"But weren't you hurt?"

"I had a few nasty cuts and bumps and a thumping headache for days. I've still got a couple of bruised ribs but provided I don't move suddenly or laugh too much, they're no problem. Sneezing left me in a screaming heap. But I'm fine now. You know me – even when I had that skiing accident, the only bone I broke was my little finger!"

Kimberley did not laugh. "Bob, this is the third car crash in two years. You've got off lightly apart from the insurance. I suppose that doesn't matter to you since it's the company that pays for it. No one can go through life being so happy-go-lucky as you. Sooner or later your luck is going to run out."

"I'm even luckier than you know. I've had five crashes. I've only admitted to Mum the ones where I haven't been able to make the other guy pay. Cyril's handled all the dealings with the insurance company for me without telling anyone. He's a real pal – I shall have to find a pretext for giving him a bonus from the company."

"I give up," muttered Kimberley. She had long ago learnt that when a personality overflows with energy, their natures thrive on impulse, change and the irrational, happily accepting the consequences of danger and defeat. "Only you can get away with things like this. And Cyril's too nice for his own good. I can't imagine him doing that for anyone else. Irene would be furious if she knew. Don't worry, I won't tell her. But I think you ought to."

"Let's see how this evening goes first. I want to see James tomorrow to get something so I won't be getting back till later – I'll get a lift back home or stay over at James's. Mum's bound to be more amenable after the funeral so I'll have a chat with her when all the fuss has died down a bit. I've failed two of my exams as well, so that's more bad news she'll have to hear. I'm happy to learn at my own pace – not that of the university."

He patted Kimberley's arm affectionately and lounged back in his seat. "That's enough interrogation, for now, Ms Spotty Muldoon. Tell me about your news. How are Richard and Anna and the dogs? Have they got nice pink spots on their chins too?"

Chapter 2

With the possible exception of her father's sudden death two years ago, Kimberley's life had been ordered, tranquil and – let's face it – boring. A bright intelligence and a warm, good nature had met few challenges, and her personal development was a predictable result of an insular and relatively privileged background. Her existence was ordered to a disturbing extent. Even her clothes were tidily separated into the type of occasion: those for work were all colour-matched and worn in strict rotation. She had well-developed routines throughout the day for efficiency and economy of mental effort. She even subconsciously divided each slice of bread into equal bite-sized pieces, while regretting that the human jaw was not conveniently square (or even hexagonal) for easier patterns of consumption. Such tidiness contrasted strangely with a hunger for new and exotic experiences with the inevitable disruption that accompanies them.

She had never experienced any sense of inadequacy of herself as a person. Her social situation, her upbringing and her easy-going personality had equipped her well. Little had troubled an orthodoxy of outlook and activities; family, friends and occupations all reflected similar values and concerns to her own.

She had been too young to be fully aware of the trauma when her parents split. Her father's business success had not been reflected in his marriage. Of the local beauties vying for his attention, he had eventually picked Shirley, fair-haired and green-eyed, with a riveting figure and mood swings to match. She learnt to resent the demands of the growing business as well as her husband's occasional dalliances with eager female programmers. Suspecting that not all the unidentified lady telephone callers were IT managers, she had slipped back into the glamorous circle of friends she had before the marriage. After the birth of Richard, more attentive lovers began to occupy her nights as well as her days. However, her discretion and David's indiscretions meant that he was truly astonished when she ran off with a fire alarm salesman a year after Kimberley was born. The houseful of water sprinklers that she had convinced David to install had failed to dampen other fiery activities. More cynical observers wondered why she hadn't let the situation run and have it all – secret lovers, money and sympathy for her apparent uncomplaining tolerance of David's sexual adventures.

But David quickly found consolation in Irene, no less pretty but somewhat more calculating than her predecessor. Taller than most, with deep auburn hair, she had magnificent dark blue eyes that lent a coquettish expression to a restless scanning of her surroundings. But when she spoke, her voice was low and charming with a kind of soft huskiness. David was entirely smitten. The couple married two months later. The consensus was that Irene was more interested in the wealth and social status the alliance gave her than in the man himself. Time modified this view. While she certainly enjoyed the family's prestige in the community, it was eventually acknowledged that she was a loyal wife and caring stepmother. David appeared to be content after his disastrous loss of face with Shirley, and he spent a little more time at home, maybe unwilling to risk another public blow to his pride.

Both adored their new baby son who combined Richard's cleverness with Kimberley's sociability. The two older children never begrudged the attention Robert attracted right from birth. Irene had pressured David to purchase Prospect Hall, and the family now lived there as Shirley had contracted multiple sclerosis and reluctantly decided that the children would be better off with their father. Besides, David had deeper pockets to pay top lawyers to plead his custody claim.

At the old mansion, life continued pleasant and comfortable – thanks to the increasing prosperity of the family business. The car crash that killed David and left Irene with a slight limp was emotionally devastating, of course, but failed to significantly disrupt the domestic and business arrangements. The dilemma over who would run Weatherby's was quickly resolved when Irene immediately asserted her newly acquired majority shareholding rights and stepped in ahead of Barry, David's younger brother. Despite having no previous relevant experience, she listened to the right people's advice, showed considerable shrewdness in controlling costs and acquitted herself astonishingly well within a year, finally earning the sincere respect, if not the affection, of friends and business colleagues.

The children had been schooled in her conventional view of the world which required that funerals should be respectfully observed, so Kimberley found it entirely fitting that next morning she should find her stepmother sitting quietly in the living room dressed in black from head to toe. Though her costly outfit was specially acquired for the occasion, Irene never looked showy, overdressed or inappropriately attired.

"Have they invited you?" she called from the kitchen.

Her mother grimaced. "No! That charming bitch – God forgive me! – would never do that but I'm going anyway."

Kimberley made no response but continued to make a cup of coffee and pour some cereal into a bowl, skirting round Anna, the Filipino au pair, who was loading the dishwasher. "Is Richard taking you?"

"No. He had to go into the office first to work on some figures for tomorrow's meeting."

"What about Bob?"

"He left early saying he had to see that new friend of his – Jonathan or Jeremiah or something." Irene was unusually vague. "Maybe it's better if he didn't come."

"His name's James," said Kimberley, but she doubted that her mother heard her. "What time is the funeral?"

"Eleven o'clock. At Saint Ninian's."

Kimberley thought carefully before she continued. "Look, I have to be here for the marquee contractors, but if it's the same guy as last year, he knows what he's doing and once they're underway, I'm sure I could leave them to it for a couple of hours – if you'd want me to come with you."

Irene was silent for a few moments then softly accepted the offer.

*****

The sun was bright if not very hot for the time of year, and some dark clouds were lurking ominously in the west, but no rain yet. As promised, Richard was waiting at the church; reliable, dull Richard. The church was filled with the great, the good and the grief-stricken (although you could easily miss the handful of those in the last category). The family squeezed into three separate seats near the back and did not have long to wait for the coffin, carried by six not-very-stalwart men – employees? – and followed by just the new widow and son, Freddie The Unsteady.

As the cortège moved along the sun-dappled nave, the congregation stood, and many people turned to look, whereupon Kimberley's eyes widened with astonishment. Nearer the front and across the nave stood Paul Panesar. Across the sea of heads and hats, he acknowledged her presence with a polite nod. Inexplicably, she once more became aware of the bright pink spot on her chin.

What on earth was he doing here? Surely there was no family or social link. And any business connection with a foreigner was unlikely. Maybe after hearing yesterday's conversation in the car, his curiosity was piqued. No! Holidaymakers – if that's what he was – don't attend the funerals of local dignitaries on a whim.

Kimberley would have failed to concentrate on the proceedings anyway. After seeing Paul in attendance, her thoughts were even less biddable. The service was exactly as expected, and excessively tedious, but no eulogy was given by the family. Lady Galbraith sat stony-faced the whole time (destined by Nature to look the part of the grieving gorgon) while Freddie squirmed periodically, whether from embarrassment, boredom or a hangover was unclear.

Kimberley studied the new heir. She had not seen him for many years. In his early thirties, he had a clear complexion with attractive regular features. A moustache and neat goatee might have added an air of refinement but this was obviated by the closely shaven head above a truculent expression. It was an overtly loutish display and out of place in such respectable company, like Jack the Ripper turning up at a Sunday School picnic.

The mourners moved outside to view the deceased begin his final journey to the crematorium and a private service for the family and invited guests only. Again, Kimberley caught sight of Paul, and he must have seen her puzzled look as he began to walk across to them. His exotic dark looks were softened by the gentle sunlight – but still arresting. And his teeth were so white and even, they had to be cosmetically enhanced. Before she had chance to decide exactly how she was going to greet him, Charlie Jenkins, one of Sir Philip's employees from way back, strode over to them, boomed a hello and shook Irene's hand vigorously. She may have been flattered by the warmth but not by the noisy enthusiasm.

Kimberley was able to step aside and greet Paul warily. What to say? Interrogating him on his reasons for being there seemed churlish, but Paul took the initiative.

"I wasn't expecting to see all your family here."

"Except Bob," Kimberley corrected. "And I cannot imagine that the mention of the funeral in the car yesterday prompted your attendance."

Paul smiled faintly but declined to answer the remark. "Quite a turnout. He must have been well-liked."

"Or simply rich and important." Kimberley immediately regretted speaking cynically of the dead. "But yes, I think he was generally liked. People are here from the mainland, I think, not just the local bigwigs."

Paul looked around solemnly. "I would like to know more about your two families' connections. Just the software business?"

"Yes, while they could agree. Since the split, there's been no direct contact but, on this island, everyone knows everyone else, so we all know what's happening."

"And the software business did very well after the two split?"

"Not sure what you're implying, but yes. It's now listed and has performed spectacularly well. However, that could change very soon."

"Why do you say that?"

Kimberley regretted making the observation but felt obliged to explain. "His son, Frederick. He's the archetypal rich man's son – wine, women and song. And drugs."

"Hmm. Very different from his partner's family."

Kimberley checked his face for sarcasm, but none was apparent so she continued, warming to the subject. "Maybe he'll change. Up till now, he hasn't spent much time on the island, but now he's inherited the family estate, he may stay here more; lovely house and grounds on the road west to Peel. But I can't see Freddie getting involved in the business. He'll probably just install a harem in the house, fill the swimming pool with vodka and smoke, snort or inject himself to heaven. Like father, like son."

"What makes you say that?" Paul asked sharply, turning his head to look at her.

"Well, Sir Philip was quite a womaniser – reputedly. Freddie fancies he is too, but he doesn't have the charm of his father, just the money. But it seems to do the trick."

"So there are no other children?" The questioning seemed relentless.

"There was a daughter, much older than Freddie, but she ran away and joined some sort of hippie group when she was nineteen or twenty, then went trekking in the Himalayas or something. Sir Philip was very cut up. She was a real beauty, they say, and the favourite. No one's heard anything from her since. Probably eaten by a yeti."

Paul had been listening attentively, prompting her to say more than she would have liked and Kimberley was starting to feel uncomfortable with all the questions. "Why all this interest? Do you have a business connection?"

There was a pause while Paul resumed his survey of the people around.

"Remotely yes. So why is your mother here at the funeral?" Paul now looked across at both Irene and the grieving widow, evidently making a judgment of both.

"Because. It's the respectable thing to do. Now Dad's dead, I suppose she thinks she ought to represent him. After all, they shared a major part of their lives. And there's the chance of mixing with potential customers. Irene doesn't miss a trick as far as business goes. Sir Philip must have had a lot of useful contacts – not just on the island. Anyway, I ought to re-join the family."

Kimberley moved back towards Irene's side and was disturbed to find Paul shadowing her. The group's initial nostalgic interchanges about the deceased, their families and the weather had been made, and Richard was breaking the mood somewhat by saying, "And how's business these days?" Charlie paused, his voice lost its heartiness, and one of his pudgy hands started to finger his ear.

"We-e-ll, not as good as it might be, that's for sure. There's not much new business around, and we're losing one or two existing customers. The trouble is that the Island's financial services industry creams off all the best talent so we don't do as much development as we should. And I don't think young Mr Freddie's the right man to sort things out – any more than his mother is. We're hoping there'll be no redundancies, but…well, we shall certainly miss the old man – God rest his soul."

Irene made appropriate consoling noises while the conversation ground to a halt as it so often does when old friends find that ancient familiarity fails to support the renewal of meaningful conversations. Unable to share the intimacy of Irene's obvious grief, Charlie stepped back and turned to move away – reluctantly, Kimberley thought. The social hiatus and space were immediately filled by the figure of Paul.

"May I introduce myself, Mrs Weatherby? My name is Paul Panesar; I had the privilege of meeting your other son Bob and Kimberley here yesterday when they kindly gave me a lift from the airport."

There was a fraught pause as if each were trying to outdo the other in social composure. Irene put out then quickly retracted her hand, obviously puzzled at his presence at the gathering and loath to evince any gesture of welcome.

"So that's why you were so late," muttered Irene as she gave the merest nod. As warm as a mortuary in winter. But Richard held out his hand to greet Paul politely.

"Your other son, Bob, was telling me about the business. You must be a remarkable woman to manage it so well."

Irene's features froze. Extending small talk with intrusive strangers – and foreign-looking ones at that – did not accord with either her present mood or the snob in her. And flattery cut no ice with her at all. *"Oh dear,"* thought Kimberley, *"this is not going well."* Desperately wanting something to divert attention from the iciness, she offered, "Richard acts as our accountant. He's not interested in cars like Bob is, but he is extremely good at minimising our tax bill."

Now Paul's eyebrows rose a fraction, and his features hinted at disapproval. Kimberley winced then thought, *"Good grief, does he think we cook the books or practise gross tax evasion? No, I don't like you, Mr Panesar. My first impression was correct."*

"Are you family?" asked Irene, noticing that he was not joining the private cortège.

"Er, no."

"Quite," murmured Irene. *"Many are called, but few are chosen."*

"There are some business connections."

"Do you live here or are you on holiday?" queried Richard, thinking to identify a potential customer.

"No." A pause. Evidently, Mr Panesar was as unwilling to furnish information as his interlocutors were. "Well, it was nice to have met you all," and he moved away.

Irene looked after him as though conversing with him was second only to root canal work then turned her attention quickly to the practical. "Are you dining with us tonight, Kimberley? I shall need to tell Anna."

Paul's departure left no residual effect apart from uneasiness in Kimberley at the lack of explanation for his attendance. And, even more curious, he had been listening intently to Charlie's remarks about the business.

"Er, no." Kimberley dragged her attention back. "I'm seeing the girls tonight and we might be going to the cinema."

Irene sighed with a trace of self-pity. "So, it's just me alone, then."

*****

Like the earlier sunshine, Kimberley's bewilderment had completely dispersed by the time she met up with her friends. It was in one of those restaurants where the tables are packed so closely together that you would need multiple limb amputations to sit in comfort, so she had difficulty wrestling herself and her umbrella across to them. She surreptitiously glanced around as she moved to check for anyone else who might know her so she could decide in advance whether to acknowledge them or not. She had become an expert in the delicate art of differentiating the feigned warmth at meeting business contacts with the genuine stuff for people she wanted to spend time with. Nevertheless, the local, albeit modest, fame fed her vanity.

Faint whiffs of a sodden humanity overlaid more tempting aromas of food; she thought she could see steam rising from the hunched bodies as from a huddle of damp and docile dogs. Typically, Julie was leaning forward in earnest discussion, her face partly obscured by a shock of thick, shiny black hair which she tossed back when she laughed or wished to add emphasis to a particularly apt remark. Lisa, dear, dumpy, fluffy-haired Lisa, was leaning back, listening attentively, lacking Julie's carefully contrived chic, but displaying the endearing qualities of a 13.5 tog duvet.

After they had all exchanged greetings, Kimberley sat down and searched the menu for a pizza rich in anti-oxidants and low in spot-inducing fat.

"And another thing," Julie tossed back her hair, reluctant to abandon her train of thought before Kimberley arrived, "do you know what those geriatric Town Commissioners have gone and done? – painted double yellow lines along the whole road! How am I going to sell my flat, when no one can park within a hundred yards of it? Brian and Cheryl upstairs are livid. No one visiting us can park nearby."

"Can they do that without giving any notice so that residents can object?" queried Lisa.

"It's quite a narrow road," mused Kimberley, "but I shouldn't have thought there was a traffic problem. Didn't anyone ask the workmen while they were doing it?"

"No one saw them. We came out this morning, and there they were – the lines, that is. They must be doing the unpopular jobs by night, these days. I'm going to the Town Hall to complain after school tomorrow anyway, Petty bureaucrats!"

"How's Shirley doing, Kim?" asked Lisa, as Julie paused to sip her drink. As a carer in a nearby nursing home, and would-be nurse, Lisa had a professional interest.

"Some days are better than others. Her main problem is boredom. Now that she's virtually confined to a wheelchair, she has too much thinking time – mostly about the events of the past because Dan-the-Man doesn't visit very often now. She seems to depend more and more on news about the family. I can understand this, and I ring her at least once a week, but I don't think Richard does. He's always saying he's busy and is always going out, but you'd think he could do that for his mother. At least he can remember her when she was at home."

"Yes," agreed Lisa, "but aren't most men like that?"

There was a pause when they would have expected Julie to cut in with some acerbic anti-men diatribe, but she remained attentive to her cutlery.

"So, girls, what do you think I should wear at the barbecue?"

"Well, as you're royalty, nothing too understated as you usually do. You need something to dazzle – sequins, gold lamé, Jimmy Choos."

"For a barbecue?"

"Ignore her," reassured Lisa, "you'll look great in anything. The only thing to worry about is the weather. After this rain, stiletto heels may not be a good idea."

"We've got a marquee just in case it rains on the day, but the ground can still be a bit soft. And I can't wear trainers – Irene would be apoplectic if I did."

"Don't you mind that?" questioned Julie. "I wouldn't want my stepmother telling me what to wear."

Kimberley smiled. "It's not quite like that. Irene's opinion is usually worth listening to and, anyway, this is a business do so she needs to know that we're presenting the right image, I suppose. She'll be more concerned with how much food is wasted. You know how she hates any sort of waste, and these barbecues stress her out. She keeps following the kids around and telling them to finish up their hamburgers."

"Rather you than me," continued Julie. "Having a family business means your life's not your own. No wonder you've tried to get away. I think Richard would like to."

"What makes you say that?" Kimberley was puzzled why Julie would know her brother's inclinations.

Julie cleared her throat. "What man wants to work with his mother? Anyhow, how's Bob, the charcoal grey sheep – or should I be asking Lisa? Looking forward to seeing him again?"

Lisa blushed. "It's not like that. Bob and I are just friends. Bob's far too young for me, and he's not interested in having just one girl. I know that, but he is fun to be with. In fact, I'm seeing him tonight."

Kimberley's face fell. "Oh, so you won't be coming to the cinema. Well, make sure you have some money to pay for the drinks as well as his taxi home. He's broke again."

"No problem this time – we're meeting at one of his friends' place. Sounds like a DVD-and-take-away, doesn't it?"

"I can't come either, Kim. Tiffany has a swimming lesson this evening."

"What about afterwards?"

"Sorry, Kim, I still can't make it – I have a date."

Lisa raised an eyebrow. "Not the same one as last week? This could be getting serious, Kim. Come on, who is it?"

Julie smiled enigmatically. "He's a ginger-haired octogenarian brain surgeon," she confided.

Kimberley looked sideways at Lisa. "Sounds quite a catch. Does he have a brother?"

Julie shrugged, not wanting to continue the conversation.

"So, I'm on my own tonight, then. Just like Irene."

Lisa looked genuinely sorry. "Why not join us, Kim? You know Bob won't mind, and there's going to be a gang of us at this guy's place because his parents are away. Come on!"

"No," she laughed, trying to appear less despondent than she felt. "Maybe Irene could do with some company."

Kimberley was in the large utility room, a few hours later, pleasantly tired, after having moved some trestle tables and folding chairs into the marquee – now successfully erected on the sweeping lawn. As she undid her trainers to change into house shoes, she looked up to see Irene standing in the doorway, enquiring about the marquee's seating layout.

Their conversation ceased when they heard a car coming up the gravel drive at the side of the house. Kimberley looked across out of the window and saw a familiar brand-new white BMW convertible. Irene looked at it, puzzled, and then her mouth tightened with a simmering resentment as she saw Bob get out of the passenger door. Both of them continued watching intently, as he exchanged a few words with the driver then walked towards the back entrance while the car reversed out and drove away.

Kimberley tried to see the driver's face, but it was difficult through the reflections in the windscreen. She went closer to the window then pulled back quickly as Bob waved cheerfully at her. Shit! How embarrassing to be caught watching them! She bent her attention back to the muddy footwear. Bob came in and greeted his mother, then obeyed her cool request to come into her study for a discussion.

Sometime later the siblings met as Bob emerged from the study looking momentarily chastened – a look which he quickly replaced with smiling optimism upon seeing his sister.

"How did it go?"

"Not so well. I must be losing my touch. I can't have another company car until I graduate and join the business. That's another two years, and I'm not sure I want to work for Weatherby's anyway." He paused and ran his hand mindlessly along the wall. Bob was a fidget.

"I'd like to go abroad and do something different, perhaps work my way round the world or study in the States. Three of the guys in my year are planning to take a year out and travel in the Far East. I was thinking of joining them. I just don't want to go back to uni right now for lots of reasons that I don't particularly want to go into. So, I'll just have to find a way to buy a new car out of my own pocket. Trouble is I've got a few debts at the moment."

"What do you do with all your money, Bob?" Kimberley knew that his allowance was generous.

Bob grinned. "Buy textbooks, of course! Seriously, it doesn't go far if you want to have any sort of social life in London. And some of the students don't have much money, so I help them out a bit. Come down and stay with me for a while and see. You'll have more fun than you're having at the moment over here, I bet! Am I right?" he queried as Kimberley smiled wryly. "I take it you haven't got yourself a new boyfriend yet."

"No, I haven't," she admitted. "I'm not sure I could trust anyone again after John running off with that –"

Bob put his arm round her shoulder. "Tart?" he suggested. "Forget him, Kim, there are plenty of fellas around who are nearly as wonderful as me" – he side-stepped quickly to avoid Kimberley pushing him back on to the stairs. "And, anyway, I bet you're thrilled to have someone to keep you company at the barbecue."

She stared in amazement. "Who?" she exclaimed.

"The wonderful Mr Paul Panesar, of course. Don't you remember?"

"With me?" Kimberley spluttered. "But you haven't told him that – not in those words."

"Yes – didn't I say that? I thought you'd be pleased. He seems a presentable guy – you know you like these smart City types, and he seems pleased to come. Probably hasn't anything better to do."

"Thank you very much!" she retorted. "You might have checked with me first. Would you believe it, he came to the funeral today and introduced himself to Irene. I've never seen her so nonplussed. Talk about Dullsville on legs! And stuck up. Not my choice for a fun time. But I'll be too busy anyway to look after such a miserable so-and-so."

"No, Kim, you've got him all wrong. He's not like that. I got on with him incredibly well on the flight. Honest, he's okay when you get to know him. You know how good I am at sussing people out. Trust me. And, anyway, who are you going to be with? By yourself? So, you can devote all your energies to looking after the deserving workers who make profits for us? *Noblesse oblige* and all that! Get a life, Kim! I promise I'll keep an eye on you to make sure you're okay. Lisa will be coming so we can make up a foursome and maybe go out together afterwards. And James and some other friends will be coming too. We can have some fun – I've already got this year's idea worked out. Come on, cheer up!"

He punched her affectionately on her arm then ran upstairs, whistling, the remonstration from his mother already forgotten. Like the beetle in the cornfield – in one ear and out the other.

Chapter 3

The only thing Kimberley disliked about estate agents was working Saturdays. You could even say she hated it. Sundays were okay although she usually had those free unless she was covering for another member of staff. She'd never found there was much she wanted to do on Sundays, and it only meant a few hours in the office anyway. Even hangovers could be managed. But Saturdays were another matter. They were always busy and very tiring, leaving her out of sorts for enjoying the high point of the week's entertainment in the evening. Parties, clubs, gigs, even just a take-away with a bunch of friends were all ideal ways of finishing the week and setting her up for the next. So, despite having taken two days' leave for the funeral and to prepare for the barbecue, she rose irritably when the alarm woke her for work at seven-thirty the next morning.

She turned on the shower of her en suite and sat glumly on the edge of her bed, the water spattering uselessly in her shower cubicle. Even though she was wide awake, she felt tired. Her eyelids felt heavy and prickly, and her body stiff and stodgy, unwilling to exhibit any of the morning's customary rush of energy that drove her to meet the day's activities. And the rain was still dripping against the window.

She stepped into the shower and reflected on yesterday's board meeting as she soaped.

It had been difficult and continued much later than usual. After the routine review of the month's figures, Irene had castigated all the managers for one reason or another. Actions were placed on everybody to provide detailed reasons for the poor figures and identify an action plan to solve the problems they reflected. Then came the latest news about the negotiations for the Indian car distribution deal which was conditional on acquiring a large parcel of adjoining land to accommodate the enhanced activities – land owned by the Galbraith family. And everyone could see the problems they were going to have with that now. Sir Philip was a reasonable man and there was every chance a deal could have been struck – albeit at a price. Now that looked doubtful.

Back at Prospect Hall after the funeral Irene had asked if she were dining in on Saturday night. Kimberley had declined even though she had no other plans as yet. Her voice was calm but inside her, deep inside, something sighed. Saturday night looked as exciting as a washing line.

"Oh," Irene was clearly disappointed. "We're having some important company with the Quirkes – he was Mayor of Douglas a few years ago, remember? – and their son George. He came back to the island a couple of months ago as the new director of the Manx Private Health Fund and, as I think I mentioned yesterday, is planning to replace all his sales fleet cars soon – for the whole UK. He also seems to have considerable influence with the Town Commissioners already which might help our plans for the business. I'd like to show them a happy, united family with Bob back. Richard will be here, of course. And Uncle Barry's coming with Ann Ingram again."

Kimberley smiled in a conciliatory fashion. "Has Barry decided to marry Ann yet, do you think? She seems very keen on the idea. A Weatherby is a good catch." She stopped abruptly as she realised the remark may have been too close to Irene's own situation all those years ago. "No, I want to go out and, frankly, I'm not in the mood for business entertaining right now. I think I need a holiday. My life's so dull at the moment, and I need something to cheer me up." Besides, she silently added, from what I've heard, George Quirke is a treacherous, randy sod who can't keep his paws off any woman. Like his father.

Kimberley dragged her thoughts back to the day ahead and sighed as she dressed and made her way down to the kitchen for breakfast. This Saturday night still needed sorting out. No way was she going to stay in for yet another night. *"I might as well be Bridget Bloody Jones! I need a life beyond work. I've got to do something."* But at least the spot on her chin was fading.

The morning passed quickly as usual, dealing with callers, arranging viewings and amending details of an expensive flat that had just come back on the market. It was almost three o'clock before she realised she was hungry. Collecting up some orders from the others, she dashed out to the sandwich bar a few doors down the road. As she waited for the order to be made up, she watched the passers-by absent-mindedly. It had started raining again but she had not brought an umbrella with her. Away from the stimulus of the office, she felt soggy and defeated. So what if her hair got wet? She wasn't going anywhere. The strange tiredness of the morning swept over her again along with the realisation that everyone else seemed to have plans to enjoy themselves tonight except her. She envied Julie's relish for attacking the problems life threw at her and Lisa's equanimity in accepting them. Kimberley seemed unable to adopt either attitude. Maybe she just needed that holiday. Despite frequently thinking of this, she had failed to organise one, obligingly providing cover for her work colleagues and constantly finding that Irene had reasons for her presence at the house. Like corporate entertaining masquerading as sociability. And the company barbecue.

Momentarily her attention was caught by the display in a travel agent she was passing on her way back to the office. *'Colourful India.'* Just the ticket! Sitting alone in front of the Taj Mahal like Princess Diana. She then became aware of a mixture of virility and aftershave next to her. The face was familiar and Kimberley responded with her customary bright "Hi!" before she realised that it was the unwelcome Mr Panesar. The disparity between her private imaginings and reality was disconcerting. She was about to quickly move on when she recalled Bob's remark about inviting him to tomorrow's barbecue. Perhaps it would be better to say a few words and see whether the invitation was going to be taken up. If so, she must contrive to discourage him without leaving a bad impression of the business. Native friendliness would be extended accompanied by indigenous guile.

"Enjoying the shops?" No response. Stuff him! "Looks like tomorrow's barbecue will be a washout, doesn't it?" He was now looking at her intently, over a collar turned up against the rain, but there was no smile. "I'm afraid I have to get back to the others – they can't work without their fix of coffee."

37

"Is that where you work?" He looked along the road to the estate agents. Kimberley nodded. "How fortunate. I need to talk to you."

"What about?"

"A flat. But let's get inside out of this rain."

So he wanted a flat. The question she most wanted to ask was `What on earth for?' but professionalism kicked in and, upon arriving at her desk after distributing the rest of the goodies, she began the process of determining his requirements: to buy or rent? – either; how big? – not bothered; where? – not sure yet; what price? – doesn't matter... *Bloody timewaster!* Kimberley turned away from her monitor, looked him straight in the eye and waited.

It took a while but they got there eventually. The idea was obviously a new one to him so the specific requirements had to be teased out of him – and even then they were subject to constant revision. However, to her delight, Julie's flat might just fit the bill. She was able to arrange an immediate viewing so, with a wistful glance back at her still uneaten sandwich, they set off through the busy Saturday traffic.

It went remarkably well despite the initial trek due to the gleaming new double yellow lines on the road immediately outside. Julie was at home and duly enumerated all the advantages and slid over the drawbacks. Not that there were many.

"So? Does this suit you?"

"Maybe. Is there no garage?"

"No. It's so central that a car is not necessary."

"Why did you park so far away?"

"Double yellow lines outside mean you cannot park there." He looked annoyed. "But you don't have a car – or does Mrs Panesar?" queried Kimberley slyly.

"No. No Mrs Panesar. And no car – yet. Do you have any other flats?"

"Several, but it won't be possible to view them this afternoon. I could arrange for you to see them next week. If you're still here."

"If I'm buying a flat it's probably that I shall be, isn't it? Unless I get poisoned at the barbecue tomorrow." A faint smile indicated it was a joke.

"Oh, so you're coming? I mean, that will be nice for you."

"Your brother has been telephoning me, insisting that I do. He seems to think that it will persuade me to buy one of your cars. But I can see that you are not so pleased with the prospect. Would you prefer I didn't?"

Kimberley gulped and swiftly adopted an exemplary professional smile. "Not at all and I'm sorry if I gave that impression. I just didn't think you would want to. It's just a crowd of ordinary families enjoying a day out. Irene started organising them a few years ago; she wanted to make our family seem more accessible, less stand-offish, though it was probably her that gave that impression in the first place."

"What happens?"

Kimberley shrugged. "Most of the men just hog the bar and talk shop but I think it helps the women feel more involved. There's a bouncy castle and a little roundabout for the kids. We tried some races for the children last year, which went down very well – egg and spoon, three-legged races, sack races – I'm sure you know the sort of thing. The food and everything is free but some of the staff organise a tombola stall for which there's a small charge, with all the takings going to a charity of their choice. It seems to work surprisingly well. We're expecting about two hundred people – if the weather holds."

"And what does Bob do?"

"Surprise us! The first time he disguised himself as a tramp and was shuffling round the garden, asking people for their burgers and hot dogs. Bob's a superb mimic, he can hit off to a tee any accent or mannerism. He looked awful, with a big unkempt beard and a battered hat and this big scruffy overcoat which smelt dreadful. Irene asked Richard to get rid of him but the next thing we knew," Kimberley could not prevent herself laughing at the recollection, "this tramp came up behind her and whispered, 'Give us a kiss, missus!' I shall never forget the look on her face! For a few moments she just couldn't speak then Bob couldn't maintain the act any longer, whipped off his hat and showed her who it was. Even when she realised the joke, she couldn't join in the laughter. Bob reckoned she was like a duchess at a thrash metal gig. She was convinced everyone would ridicule her."

"And did they?"

"Of course not. Everyone thought it was a terrific joke. The next year he hired a pantomime horse costume with a friend and went round trying to pinch the food again. The children loved it. Of course, Irene knew it was him this time so although she was a bit anxious, she accepted that it made things a bit more fun."

A faint but distinct smile was hovering over Paul's face. "And since then?"

"He and a group of school friends dressed up as Morris dancers – displaying some original variations. Last year he was at university in London so didn't have time to organise much. Halfway through the afternoon, he announced that there would be a beauty contest – Miss Lovely Legs of Weatherby's and persuaded several men to be judges – then apologised, claiming he'd misread the programme and the contest was *Mister* Lovely Legs. So all the 'judges' were now contestants and had to roll up their trousers and parade around and the one that got the loudest cheer from the ladies won a bottle of whisky. A young apprentice mechanic won it – then dropped it getting out of his car on the way home, so he never got to enjoy it."

"What's he doing this year?"

"I don't know – no one does. It'll be different, that's for sure."

At last he smiled openly. "It sounds fun. I'd like to come – if you're certain it will be okay with your stepmother. I'll look forward to seeing you there. Goodbye."

His patronising tone riled her. Had she been in one of her customary cheerful moods she would have been content to leave the encounter sinking to the floor between them. But right now she needed to be in control and make something happen.

"But don't you want a lift? It's all part of the service."

Now he laughed outright. "Oh, no, I'm not going to inconvenience you again! It was very kind of you before. But I'm sure that finding my way around will be good for me. And despite your family's conviction, I'm perfectly able to organise my life. Now, which is the best way back to the hotel?"

"But this is a business arrangement, not a personal invitation."

"Look, what is it about lifts with your family? If it means that much to you okay, I'm not going to fight with you. Not here, anyway. Just lead on."

*****

Kimberley's satisfaction at winning the argument dissipated, as she drove Paul back and finished her day at the office. A mood of unrelieved gloom settled on her as she drove home. The sole redeeming feature of dull Saturday evenings was that they eliminated Sunday morning hangovers, not a very valuable attribute right now. She mulled over how this uninspiring situation had arisen.

The relationship with John had been a comfortable but rather passionless affair but it had occupied most Saturday nights and still allowed occasional more exciting activities. Since his unexpected (or was it?) departure, Kimberley had had to work hard to ensure her weekends did not drift by in solitary tedium. Sure, there were always plenty of offers and male company – of a sort – was never hard to find. The trouble was that on the island, everyone knew everyone else – of any consequence, anyway. So she relied on visiting her mother or friends on the mainland or discovering some event that needed her presence. This technique was wearing thin. Recently the long hours at work had absorbed both her energy and attention, and she rarely made specific arrangements, assuming that one or both of her friends would provide a solution. Right now, this wasn't happening. For maybe the first time in her life, Kimberley had doubts about her social adequacy.

She currently pursued no hobbies. She and John had been members of a local film club and enjoyed watching cult foreign films. Now, even though his amatory initiative had taken him to the dizzy metropolis of Llandudno, Kimberley didn't want to mix with people who had known them as a couple. She let work increasingly dominate her life and was finding that Irene promptly tried to commandeer any remainder. But then, why was the world not beating a path to her charming, well-connected door? She was clever – not brilliant, like Bob, or methodical like Richard, but far from stupid. She had no social drawbacks, no nasty private habits nor lurid skeletons in her family cupboard. Money was not a problem. And her appearance was, well, okay. Mousy hair, nondescript features – the sort you could see everywhere, three on every bus – but a reasonable shape.

Kimberley's self-image lay somewhere between the contrived, angular chic of Julie and the warmth of rumpled, voluptuous Lisa. She never credited the sunshine laying golden slivers through her hair, the merry, honeyed-hazel eyes and legs as long as the names of obscure Welsh villages. She could never see what others noticed – a lithe, elfin quickness and a sparkling, silvery laugh, quite at odds with her determined nature. She was a nicer person in consequence. No one becomes more attractive by having a full inventory of their assets.

She crept up to her room so that Irene would not notice her low-spirited return. Then her mobile phone rang.

"Lisa says you're not doing anything tonight." It was Bob.

"Irene's got a dinner party." She hoped she'd remembered her cover story accurately.

"Yeah! And you can't think of anything you'd rather do except watch stones wrestle. Come over, Kim. There's a gang of us. We've got music, food and drink – besides, James wants to meet you. The address is…"

Kimberley noted the address and hung up after being commanded to be there in half an hour. Another time, she would have dismissed the offer of spending an evening with Bob's friends. But tonight…

The unexpected diversion had lent her energy for a quick shower and a change of clothing. If she were going to meet someone for the first time, she may as well impress them. So on with the tight leather trousers, designer tee shirt and some flimsy, strappy heels that had lain in the back of the wardrobe since that awful evening when John had taken her to one of his friend's parties. Ugh! What a night! Just imagine a roomful of teachers, most of them forty-something, sitting around (they couldn't even sustain enough energy to stand, for heaven's sake) discussing earth-shattering matters like patrolling the playground for questionable substances and the latest approach to teaching fractions.

She turned into the quiet, leafy avenue whose name was written on the slip of paper on the seat beside her. The house name was etched on the stone pillars either side of a long gravel driveway. Kimberley parked in the road but did not get out immediately. She wanted to sit for a few moments and collect her thoughts. The evening ahead did not offer inordinate pleasure, but it did offer interest by meeting new people and the satisfaction of a performance to impress Bob's intriguing new friend. The actress inside her glanced down at her outfit with approval, adjusted her shoe straps to the most comfortable position and opened the car door with a grand

and careless flourish. She carefully stepped down over the gravel and through the drizzle towards a large, gracious Victorian house. She went up to the door, rang the bell and applied her most charming smile.

When the door opened, everything in the world seemed suddenly changed.

"You're Kimberley!" A hunk of sun-blond hair and golden-brown eyes radiated a warm engulfing caress over her entire body. Unbidden, her smile moderated to a disconcerting admiration in response.

"Hello," she murmured. He extended his hand encouragingly – she needed it like Justin Bieber needed hair restorer – but as soon as she reached out in return, he took hers and raised it to his mouth, kissing it gently before slowly releasing it.

Kimberley's knees went weak at the touch of his lips. She stared down at her fingers, amazed that they appeared no different, then looked quickly back at that face as if there were only a finite time for such gazing and her soul had no time to lose trying to satisfy a new and insistent hunger.

"Come in." He stepped back to invite her in, as if into a distant land where vistas are draped in fresh colours, where new promises hint at still more unexplored places. "Bob promised me you were special and for once he didn't exaggerate. Let's get you a drink so we can get better acquainted."

There was no hesitation. "I'd adore one!" she murmured as she moved forward into the entrance hall, turning a little to look back at him as he closed the door behind her. He was wearing tight, light blue jeans and a white shirt that was beautifully filled by broad shoulders, well-muscled arms and a toned flat stomach…her eyes continued downwards avidly. Then she blinked, shook her head briefly to regain her usual composure and set her gaze in the direction he was indicating, where voices could be heard, Bob's among them.

She advanced with James close behind her, his arm hovering around her waist to guide her along a wide hallway then to the right. She was at one end of a massive kitchen. She knew professionally that the neighbourhood was well-to-do, but a glimpse into the interior was informative and intriguing. The kitchen seemed full of every culinary gadget known to man – or woman. Before her stood an oversized table covered with tangled heaps of electronic gadgetry and cabling. Various other pieces lay on the floor and on the surrounding work surfaces, interspersed with six-packs of lager and bottles of wine. Bob and two other young men were leaning across the table, discussing the connection of two huge speakers to an amplifier. Lisa and another girl were lounging opposite them on a faded upholstered sofa against the wall, wine glasses in their hands. Kimberley smiled across at them.

"Hi, Kim – be with you in a tick," called Bob. "We're just in the middle of something."

"Don't trouble yourself, she's in good hands. I'm just getting her a drink," cut in James. "What would you like – some wine? We've got all kinds. Red or white?"

Kimberley was about to say, "No thanks, I'm driving." But she heard in her mind the responses: *there was lots of time, the evening was young, one drink wouldn't matter.* And, of course, they were right. One drink, maybe two or three, wouldn't matter. And if she got drunk, so what? She could get a taxi. She looked at the back of Bob's head and recalled his instruction to her to loosen up. Okay, she would.

Then she laughed at the absurdity that having a few drinks constituting 'loosening up'. What a sad person she had become!

"White, please."

"Chardonnay, Muscadet, Prosecco, Sauternes?"

"That Chardonnay would be fine," she smiled. He poured a tumblerful. `Hmm,' she thought, *"I won't need very many of them to get drunk."* But she said nothing and took the glass from him.

"Refreshment for the body…that for the soul, well, another time," he murmured before swinging round and saying loudly, "Does anyone else want topping up?" He then walked over to add to the unknown girl's glass, before emptying the rest of the bottle into his own. He held out his glass towards Kimberley. "To what shall we drink?"

Kimberley didn't need to think for long. "To a fresh start!"

James raised his eyebrows a little and smiled approvingly. Kimberley noticed Bob's merry blue eyes glance up at her briefly before continuing his discussion with the other two guys. "To a fresh start!" echoed James.

"Now let me introduce you," he continued. "Beside Lisa is Diane, my sister. The peculiar fella with the ponytail is Dave, and the intelligent looking nerd with specs who's just about to get punched on the nose for arguing with your brother is Craig. But you can ignore both of them if you like, and talk to me, I'm the only one not still hungover from last night, anyway, so my conversation is bound to be better."

With a hand around her waist, he guided her to a pair of Windsor chairs, at the end of the table. "Now, it seems that you are looking for some improvement in your life at the moment. What can we arrange for you?" He grinned appealingly with golden brown eyes flashing an invitation to a bundle of unimaginable delights.

"Sunshine!" called Bob, "because if we use this in the rain, we're going to get electrocuted! This, Kim, is our public address system for the barbecue. James is organising one for us. I've persuaded him to give us a very good price –"

"Like the car?" she interjected.

"– like the car" – so James did get it at a knock-down price, she thought, "with special reductions for everyone that dies by electrocution."

Kimberley's mind switched to Irene's response to this. "Just how much is this going to cost?"

"Don't worry!" cut in Diane. "Money isn't everything. The most important thing is that people enjoy themselves. The cost is irrelevant."

The sentiment was worthy, but it jarred, coming from someone who had plenty. Kimberley had dealt with enough cash-strapped couples seeking an affordable home to make her appreciate the stress that lack of money entailed.

"Remember what a job it was to round up all the little kids last year? You'll be able to use this tomorrow and really boss them about. Here, where's the mike?" Diane reached out to pick it up from the floor and passed it across to him. "Have a try!"

James took it from Bob and held it close to her mouth. "You turn it on by this switch," he explained. "Now say something."

She studied the hand that was holding it – a slender, shapely hand. Except for its size and very short nails, it might have been a woman's. "Hello." She jumped as her voice boomed back at her.

"*Merde!* Volume down a bit, Craig!" called James. "Now try again."

"Hello, boys and girls. I want ten pairs, each of one boy and girl for a wheelbarrow race. Uncle Bob and Lisa will show you how it's done. Then they'll show you how to run a sack race only we're having a variation with two people in the sack at the same time – that will be fun, won't it?" She broke off giggling as Bob looked at her in astonishment and Lisa lowered her gaze in embarrassed amusement.

"James, we need to talk about this. If my beloved sister destroys my impeccable reputation with this device," he went on in mock seriousness, "I shall insist on full reparation, with damages, failing which…"

"Don't worry, Bob. If Kimberley does anything untoward, I'll put her over my knee and spank her."

Kimberley spluttered over her wine. "Like hell you will," she protested, while considering the possibility.

"Sounds good to me, James. I'll hold her down for you!"

Kimberly laughed. The banter was refreshing to her. And it was nice to get some attention. She began to relax.

James cut in. "It's wonderful to meet Bob's older sister at last. I didn't realise what he'd been hiding all this time. You can see what excellent company we can offer, and I can supply absolutely anything else you could want. We'll be organising something to eat once Einstein and Edison over there shock themselves into sobriety – the other socket, Dave. You'll fuse the microphone circuit like that!"

Seated between James and Diane, Kimberley chatted casually with them, listened to the surrounding discussions and felt comfortable with their easy friendliness. She had sipped half her wine when it was topped up by James, opening another bottle from the fridge and going round to make sure everyone's glass was full. The evening turned into night, but the group's spirits remained lively as they continued joking, working on the PA system, drinking and eventually organising a take-away Chinese meal. Kimberley noticed that Lisa quietly contributed Bob's share of the cost.

Kimberley's memories of the rest of the evening were vague. Her wine glass showed a remarkable likeness to the widow's cruse of oil. Her mind became confused, but she did recall saying that she must have some black coffee before driving home. Then Bob had to stay on – to finish something he said – so she had crawled up to one of the empty bedrooms to rest until he was ready. The next thing she knew was waking with a splitting head to find the sun high in the sky and shining through windows where she had not closed the curtains.

Chapter 4

She lay a few moments to get back her orientation. God, her head hurt. What time was it? She found she was lying on her tummy with one of her feet wedged against the bed's headboard. Her neck was stiff from lying so awkwardly and she struggled to raise her head to read her watch. Nine o'clock. It had been a long time since she had slept so late. A pity she felt no better for it. She glanced at herself in the mirrored robe doors. A mistake. Men get up looking pretty much the same as when they went to bed; women deteriorate. Not even Helen of Troy could have looked good at first light.

Then she remembered it was the day of the barbecue. Irene would have long been up and fussing about, worrying where the rest of the family was and no doubt complaining to Richard about the two younger ones.

She heard some noises downstairs, slipped on her shoes and tottered gingerly downstairs to see who was awake. She hoped that James' parents had not returned sooner than expected.

All the others were up except Craig, who, it seemed had gone out at dawn in an attempt to drive home and been found asleep on the lawn cuddling a traffic cone. Its origin and purpose were quite unknown. After some noisy vomiting in the downstairs loo he was now slumbering peacefully on the sofa in the corner of the cavernous kitchen, totally unaware of the surrounding activity. A cat had put in an appearance and was somehow peacefully curled up on his legs.

"Good morning Kimberley. Some coffee? Breakfast?" suggested James, cradling her with a smile. Her heart just melted with delight.

"He makes a good cup of coffee, Kim. And his black pudding with scrambled eggs just hits the spot," commented Bob.

"I hope you've all made your beds this morning," said James with a convincing seriousness – until Kimberley caught sight of a suppressed smile.

"What bed?" grumbled Dave. "All I got was a sleeping bag!"

"I offered you mine, Dave," taunted Diane.

"Yes, darling, but he didn't want the bag that went with it!" sniggered Bob, unkindly. "Give the guy a break – he was tired!"

"Thank you, Bob. Remind me to crush *your* bag and its contents some time!" Diane regarded the gathering with indifference, if not contempt. She was dressed with impeccable style and full-on make-up; no trace of a heavy night. Kimberley experienced a sudden and intense aversion to this sister.

"Ignore him – he just can't recognise an angel when he meets one," whispered Dave, just audibly. Diane's expression melted with obvious pleasure at the remark.

"Dear God, is she so susceptible to flattery?" thought Kimberley. *"Or is she so stupid that she believes it?"*

"*Merde!* No milk for the coffee!" announced James. "Who's had all the milk, you guys?"

"Not me!" chorused everyone except Bob.

"Sorry, but I didn't fancy pilsner on my cornflakes," he complained drily. "They go soggier quicker."

"But you said you had scrambled eggs and black pudding," observed Kimberley.

"He had the cornflakes for supper," explained Lisa. "Two big bowls full. And then spilt half of them in the bed!" She stopped abruptly and looked across at Kimberley sheepishly.

"*Aha!*" thought Kimberley, "*so you are sleeping with Bob despite your denial last Wednesday. No surprise there.*" But it would gain her nothing to comment on it. Aloud, she said that she liked her coffee black anyway – but not her breakfast puddings.

James served the coffee and produced a packet of chocolate hobnobs. Even the faint smell of chocolate made Kimberley's stomach go into spasm. She averted her eyes and looked at Craig, still blissfully asleep on the sofa with the cat. Then she watched in amazement as the others steadily munched through them. "*How do they do it?*" she thought. "*Up most of the night drinking then perky as puppies the next morning.*"

"Well, Bob and I must be going, or Irene will be having a fit of terminal hysterics."

Bob obligingly took the hint and swiftly finished his coffee. "Yes, that's what women do when people give them problems – find relief in tears. Men prefer to masturbate. I need to get some things ready before I go back to London. I've done enough work on the PA system. Craig will be able to check it all out when he wakes up. Coming Lisa? It's okay for Lisa to have a lift, Kim, isn't it? I'll drive if you want. Damn! No, I can't, can I?" He wandered towards the front door.

Lisa ran upstairs to collect her jacket and handbag, Diane wandered outside, leaving Kimberley with James, Dave and a sleeping Craig. She looked at James shyly, wishing her head allowed her to say something appropriate. Nothing came to mind.

James smiled sympathetically. "You know you had a lot to drink last night. You're not used to it, are you? Do you want another cup of coffee before you go?"

Kimberley shook her head. She now felt rather foolish. What must he think of her?

"You'll be fine as the day progresses. And I'll see you at the barbecue – I hope. Perhaps we can get to know each other a little more."

"Yes, and when you've sorted out the public address system, you can help me with the camel rides! We plan to use some friends' horses – with a little, er, anatomical embellishment, so to speak!"

James grinned. "On condition that I can have you as a partner in the pair sack race!"

Kimberley demurred. Inventing that event may have been a tactical error. Sunday morning hangovers made stupid jokes look like just that – stupid. The impression she must have made was not what she had intended. She excused herself to look for a mirror to see the state of her clothes, face and hair. She would have to make time to freshen up at home.

She held out her hand to James to bid goodbye, but this time, after taking her hand, he slipped the other arm around her shoulders, drew her close to him and softly kissed her cheek. She smelt his fresh skin and felt his warm sweet breath against her face. Instinctively she turned, hoping he would place another kiss on her lips but he merely smiled enticingly, silently slid his hand over her hair and gently let her go. The other two bid their host and other guest goodbye. Bob then rushed outside and came back in with some branches of a fuchsia bush, which he laid as a funerary offering on Craig's chest, much to the disgust of the cat.

The three of them walked to the car and drove off, making a detour to take Lisa home. Kim could not help noticing the intense goodbye kiss, excavating each other's throats as if for a practice tonsillectomy. But Bob would not be drawn into discussing the relationship. "You look pretty rough, Kim," he said in counter to her question.

"That's just how I feel. My stomach and head keep trying to change places. What have you got planned for this barbecue today? Anything to do with the PA system?"

"Nope."

"Will you be in disguise again?"

"I'm not telling you. Wait and see."

"Does Lisa know?"

"Nope. Though I may need her help."

"To do what?"

"Stop asking questions. You're such a bossy big sister!"

Is that how people thought of her, Kimberley wondered: bossy? She considered asking Bob what she could do to improve her life, but not now. Instead, her thoughts returned to the Adonis she had just met and asked, "How did you meet James?"

"Tennis club. He joined last year when his parents moved over here from France. His father got a large payoff from selling his business."

"Strange that they haven't penetrated the island's social network."

"They seem to spend most of their time overseas. Can't see why they moved here unless it's for tax."

"What does James do?"

"Very little, as far as I can see! A man after my own heart! No, seriously, he helps out his father who's involved with an electronics group, Global Microdongles or something equally meaningful. James got a first in Physics at Imperial and then did a Master's at Warwick."

"Sounds bright. How old is he, then?"

"Older than me. Tremendously old. Really ancient. Nearly twenty-five. Even older than you – ouch! That hurt! You can't be feeling that bad to punch like that. Maybe drinking improves you. Oh, no! We've forgotten something!" he exclaimed. Kimberley hastily checked the rear-view mirror then braked to a standstill. Bob looked in the back. "I was right – we've left your Zimmer frame at James'." He nudged her arm. "Smiled a bit then, did we? Beginning to feel better?"

Kimberley grinned as they set off again. She could not help enjoying his company. He was the only person between whom and herself there were ties not just of familial affection, but unselfish reliance and protection all at the same time.

"Kim, I've got to ask you something." He picked nervously at some yellow paint on his jeans.

"What?"

"You know I'm broke. Can you lend me a couple of hundred quid?"

This was not an unusual request. On previous occasions she would remonstrate with him, argue, ask why he needed it then probably agree to lend only fifty pounds against a promise of repayment by a specific date. This morning, she felt differently. Her way of conducting her life didn't seem to have worked very well. Maybe Bob's irresponsible and profligate habits were no worse than her own careful, calculated and controlled way of life. Being prudent no longer seemed a praiseworthy virtue.

"Sure," she smiled.

Bob was astounded by her response. "Bloody hell! That was easy. What I meant was that I needed five hundred…"

"Oh no, sunshine! I wasn't so drunk last night that I can't think straight this morning. Two hundred it is. But you don't have to repay it. Just remember you owe me a favour."

Bob looked aggrieved. "Do you feel you have to say that, Kim? Have I ever let you down?"

Kimberley didn't need time to reflect on this. "No. Never," she answered quietly. "I shouldn't have said that."

Bob smiled and squeezed her arm. "That's what kid brothers are for! And to relieve you of your money! I'll tell you what – as a thank you I'll buy a giant economy-sized lot of Clearasil, 'cos it's not going away, is it?"

They drove on in friendly silence. The day was improving.

*****

Prospect Hall lay back a little from the road. Built in the early twentieth century it combined Edwardian elegance with a traditional dignity. It was distinguished by both its size and its style, particularly the elegant façade in white-rendered brick with an interesting, irregular outline and multiple windows. A lengthy gravel drive brought the visitor up the slope from the road then ran for some fifty yards between rowans and fuchsia bushes until it broadened before the main entrance, set at the side of the building. This was an imposing affair, with four wide steps flanked by sturdy columns linked to the house by low stone balustrades.

Inside there was a quiet charm, no fuss, no elaborate decoration since its construction. Rooms were tastefully furnished with elegant rugs reducing the echoey sounds from the bare, polished wooden floors. Despite the lofty hallway and corridors, there was an air of cosiness and comfort in the living rooms, maybe because it had absorbed generations of children's games, quarrels, laughter and pleasures over its century of life. Family intimacy had seeped into the structure, permeating the walls, mellowing the fabrics and softening any angularities.

In winter, the view from the front windows encompassed the grounds down to the road and then across the shallow valley to the distant fields, hedges and dwellings on the southern slopes opposite. In summer, the rich green foliage of the intervening trees showed only the dull grey-green of the far hills to be visible from the upper storey. The leafy screen lent privacy to the lawn which extended from the modest flower beds surrounding the house to the final gradual descent to the road.

This morning, the greenery shone in the sunlight as once again, the weather decided to be kind to the Weatherby staff barbecue. The ground was still damp, but a light breeze and the bright warmth of the sun promised to continue to dry it out as the day wore on.

The barbecue was due to begin at midday and, as the time approached, a trickle of people started to arrive. Kimberley was engrossed in checking the number of croquet mallets for Richard when Julie rushed up and hugged her, whooping with delight as she thrust under Kimberley's nose a hand adorned with a large diamond solitaire ring.

"Oh, no! I don't believe it. Engaged – not to the ginger-haired octogenarian brain surgeon."

"No. My fiancé's *here.!"*

Kimberley looked around to identify this brave man, but she could only see a few family groups with children and Richard, setting out the croquet hoops, who was now grinning sheepishly.

A look of shock washed over Kimberley's face. "Not Richard! *Richard!* You're joking! Oh, Julie, congratulations! Come here, Richard, you dark horse!"

"I decided we needed some more help with the sports, Kim, and the only way I could persuade her was to ask her to marry me."

"And I thought you were a modern, sensible girl! So this is the mysterious man you were dating. I'm afraid I shan't be able to buy a sympathy card before tomorrow. And we never guessed. Wait till Lisa hears about this. Or have you told her?"

"No," said Richard, "you're the first person we've told. Please don't say anything to anyone yet. We want to see Irene first. Please keep it quiet till then." The two wandered off towards the house while Kimberley slipped easily into the familiar role of the hostess, greeting the guests, pointing out the amusements and ushering them towards the food and drinks. She managed to spend a few moments watching Bob clinging halfway up a newly erected flagpole carrying two loudspeakers, shouting frantic instructions to Dave and Craig who were clustered at a discreet distance. Since no disaster seemed imminent and the later guests were happily following the early arrivals, she turned her attention to organising the camel rides.

One thing she quickly realised was that piling cushions on the backs of two unwilling ponies to represent them as camels just did not work. The creatures certainly got the metaphorical hump but the literal hump was a complete failure. After the second child thudded down onto the lawn, she was obliged to discontinue her efforts. The two victims were compensated with hugs and lollipops in the hope that the parents would not sue and Irene rapidly reclaimed the cushions, muttering dark phrases like 'health and safety' and 'insurance policy'.

As the tempting odours from the barbecue drifted across the lawn, Kimberley resorted to conventional pony rides, her disappointment dissipating when she noticed James's white convertible pull into the parking area between the minibuses laid on for the revellers. Then her disappointment was speedily reinstated when she saw Bob approaching with Paul Panesar.

To be fair, when dressed casually, he did look extremely attractive and his manner was irreproachably polite. He made several complimentary remarks about the arrangements during the ensuing chatter while Bob persisted in trying to persuade him to hire a car from Weatherby's. Evidently he now also knew that Paul was planning to stay around for a while on the island. They wandered away, Bob still engaged with his sales pitch, but not before Paul mentioned that he would be getting in touch with Kimberley next week for some more viewings. While the prospect of further uninspiring meetings did not fill her with unfettered joy, the increasing probability of a sales commission certainly did.

A surge of delight pierced through her struggles with the chubby little jockeys when she saw James wander over to her.

"Come to laugh at my efforts?"

"Not at all. Admire them, rather."

She trotted away alongside Corky and his latest aspiring rider. "You cannot believe how tiring it is even when it's not you that's doing the riding," she called back. A few moments later the trio returned.

"So last night hasn't affected your performance."

"A few glasses of wine never did me any lasting damage. My stomach wants to be somewhere else but apart from that, I'm fine. How about you?"

James smiled. He reached out and touched the sleeve of her gold-coloured tee-shirt. "This colour brings out the gold in your hair – did you know that? Or perhaps, it's the sunshine. Either way, you look like a vision in gold. A real golden girl. Twenty-four carats," he murmured.

"Thank you," she replied lamely, somewhat astonished at the flowery fulsomeness. She'd always reckoned that her hair was the colour of muddy sand. Or sandy mud. Her embarrassment prompted her to change the mood. "How's the sound system going? I noticed Bob was in pole position."

"Yes, we're having some difficulty with him as he insists on practising his Tarzan impressions, but no one's been electrocuted yet."

"Who's doing the announcing? You? Bob?"

"Neither of us. Bob says he's persuaded your elder brother – Richard. Bob has assured him that the experience will equip him for a job as a bingo caller in Blackpool. Look, I'm sorry but I'm not going to be able to stay because I have a business meeting. I'm really sorry. Especially as you look so radiant."

Kimberley had her doubts about the veracity of the compliment.

"But what are you doing this evening?"

Kimberley's face fell as she explained that she did not feel able to excuse herself from the supper Irene had planned for family and key helpers.

"So what about next Saturday?" James persisted. "I bet you don't spend every Saturday night in with the family – I know your brother doesn't! Would you like to join us? We're probably going to Benny's, that new nightclub. One of my friends is part owner and he assures me it's a great night out."

"I'd love to come!" she accepted eagerly. And the parting kiss on the cheek before he left to find Bob was some consolation for the truncated encounter.

The day progressed. By now Julie had rounded up wooden spoons, hard-boiled eggs, bin liners and short lengths of rope for the kiddies' races. She took over helping with the rides leaving Kimberley free to rush inside the house and quickly microwave a pizza for her lunch. Nowadays, she avoided eating the barbecue food. Unlike her late husband, Irene's parsimony trumped her philanthropy, and she provided only the cheapest of ingredients. Kimberley then began to organise the novelty sports which Richard was announcing on the public address system without any electrocution. These went wholly satisfactorily but left Kimberley wondering what surprise Bob was going to spring this year. She did not have to wait long. As the final wheelbarrow race between co-opted parents came to a boisterous and noisy finish, Richard, once again fearless of electrocution, commandeered the microphone and with some initial hesitation announced, "Ladies and gentlemen, we now have a special treat for you. After a lengthy search, we have been able to locate a very famous person – the confidante of the stars, the one and only Gipsy Gladys!"

He tried to lead some applause but with no success. "Gipsy Gladys has agreed to offer us her unique skills and tell our fortunes using the tarot cards. So if you have a problem or just want an insight into your future, do come and consult her, absolutely free. You will find her just inside the main entrance of the house, sitting in the hall, but of course, she can only see you one at a time. Her consultations will start in five minutes. Just form an orderly queue by the door."

So this was it. Bother! Kimberley would have liked to go and check out Bob's disguise immediately. A hand was laid on her arm. She turned to see Irene.

"This isn't good, Kimberley. Bob shouldn't meddle with the occult. He's playing with fire. It's not a just a game, you know. There are dark forces around which can have a profoundly disturbing effect." She glanced up at the sky as if checking that some vengeful deity was not planning to launch a thunderbolt or two to express disapproval at the proceedings.

Kimberley was astonished at the strength of Irene's anxiety, notwithstanding her customary religious leanings. This was a facet of her stepmother she had never seen before. "You don't believe in it, do you? That anyone actually does have psychic powers?"

"I don't know. I don't want to know. Maybe they do, maybe they don't. But some individuals who dabble with the occult become neurotic and unhappy – even if the predictions are harmless. It's playing with fire. Don't humour him."

Kimberley murmured her acquiescence then started collecting up the props from the completed sports with a bemused look.

After a few moments' hesitation, an enormous group of women plus a few bewildered men had gathered in front of the house in excited expectation. Kimberley was exasperated that such a bogus item could attract so much interest. But she was curious as to what the punters thought about their readings. After the first few emerged, she moved nearer and overheard a variety of reactions – "amazing", "very vague", "spot-on", "anyone could say that…"

The crowd did not seem to diminish so she went to see how Lisa was getting on with the ponies. A few dedicated girls were still begging rides but it was clear that people were drifting off home by now and most of the interest had been satisfied. They gave final turns then began to unsaddle the animals. Lisa offered to lead them back to their paddock at the back of the house leaving Kimberley the opportunity to sample Bob's latest prank. Not that any sister wants to hear what their brother says about them, but she wanted to see what he was doing – and how he did it.

Only one woman with a toddler was still waiting. After a few minutes, to Kimberley's amazement, Julie stepped out, looking around warily. Her face was drained of colour.

"She knew!"

"Knew what?"

The other woman was ushered inside but looked back eagerly to find out what secret had been revealed.

"About the engagement! I'd taken my ring off so that wasn't a clue. She didn't actually say the word, but she predicted the wedding. Even the actual month we'd got planned! It was unbelievable. Richard *must* have told her somehow. And there were other things she said…"

"Like what?"

Julie shrugged vaguely. "Oh, other things. I must beware the colour yellow which is giving me trouble at home, for example. I just don't know what to make of it." She hurried off in search of Richard, declining to reveal more.

Kimberley was intrigued but was too eager to try her luck rather than chase after her. She waited impatiently, cynicism giving way to curiosity.

At last Craig appeared at the door. "Are you the last one?" he asked. "I'll go and see if she's ready," then he disappeared back inside.

"He's gone to tell Bob. That's how they're working it," she thought. Craig returned and led her inside, out of the mellow sunshine and into an enveloping murk.

Chapter 5

The hall was large so that the dark wood of the doors, stairway and panelling beneath the dado rail did not usually make it dark or oppressive, just rich and warm in the light from the windows either side of the door. The stairway rose on one side, but after some half dozen steps, turned a right angle then turned again back on itself before reaching the first-floor level. The area enclosed by the first half landing usually contained an antique desk, one of several pieces Irene had inherited. This had now been moved out, and several brightly coloured blankets were draped over the banisters, stretching across to a carved wooden screen so that a small booth was formed. The gap left as the entrance was dark, and Kimberley could see nothing inside. She prayed that neither the desk, screen nor anything else had been damaged.

"How long will it take?" she asked Craig in a whisper.

"About five to ten minutes. It does vary, though. Some people have more things going on in their life than others."

"So mine won't take long. Have any men been in?"

"Two did, but neither seemed impressed. I don't know why they bothered. Or maybe they didn't like what they heard!"

Kimberley now had mixed feelings as she entered the familiar hallway. She cautiously pushed to one side a crimson blanket to enter the booth, uncertain what she would find. There was a distinct but nice smell – perfume? – it was too nice for aftershave. Nice touch, Bob. A table covered in faded floral chintz separated her from the figure hunched at the back. She – or he – was draped in shiny, dark-coloured stuff with a navy-blue woollen shawl thrown over the head, obscuring the face by deep shadow. The hands, devoid of any rings and barely visible under deep cuffs, lay folded on the edge of the table. Before them, lay a pack of large tarot cards, face down on a square of red silk.

There came a wavering, high-pitched voice.

"Sit down. Do you want a reading? Have you consulted the tarot before?"

"No – you know I haven't."

"Just relax. Breathe slowly and deeply. Exclude all other distractions. Before I do a reading, I choose the significator – the card that I feel identifies the person in front of me. For you, the significator is the Queen of Swords."

The voice was now lower and breathy, as though come from deep inside the speaker. Bob was doing this very well.

"What does that mean?"

The figure sighed. "Swords express activity, change, progress, maybe conflict. The Queen has been betrayed, deserted. But she is not one of life's passive victims. She is a woman of courage and achievement. Now I want you to shuffle the cards for me…"

Kimberley felt mesmerised as she was instructed on technique and ways to focus her concentration. She had stopped smiling cynically as she picked up the cards and shuffled them meditatively as required. Her first thoughts concerned the figure in front of her. The voice was disguised, of course. It was strained and uneven at times from the effort. The intonation and phrasing were strange. Bob was a master of dissembling to achieve this. Or was it Bob? She leant to look more closely at the face but could only glimpse a shadowed cheek before Gipsy Gladys pulled a dark scarf up over the lower half of her face to prevent any further scrutiny.

"Keep looking at the cards. Direct your thoughts at them, not me. Let your mind become quiet, so I can make a connection with your essence."

Kimberley switched her gaze and attention back to the cards. As the figure's hands reached out to take the cards and place them on the table, she felt a shock – almost scary. *The hands were not Bob's.* They looked female with long, slender fingers and neatly manicured nails. So who was it? *"Let's play along,"* she thought. *"Game or not, let's see what someone else has to say to me."* Her mood had now changed from one of scepticism to one of intense curiosity. She wanted – no, *needed* some answers. Over the last few days, she had decided that Bob's approach to life seemed fundamentally more rewarding than her own. Maybe this was fate offering guidance. Right on cue!

There followed a bewildering process of cutting, gathering and supposedly cryptic placing of the cards, accompanied by a weird, mystifying commentary. Then a long silence. From time to time the hands fluttered gracefully over the display, touching a card, then moving back, lifting another, but always replacing it in the same position. The husky voice spoke again.

"The cards are mixed. They show confusion, activity, a journey, forces pulling in different directions, like a thunderstorm that sweeps the heart with terrifying power." There was a long pause, "Love has brought you to me, but you are not love's puppet buffeted by chance. Look – these cards are reversed. There is some negativity here. You are unhappy, at a crossroads, not knowing how to move forward. But you can effect change and face the challenges that change may bring. You will need fortitude over the next few months, but do not be afraid. Before you lie obstacles, trials, happenings. Have no fear – you will be safe. All these are part of the cycle of change."

The figure paused, and the voice became even lower. "You must remember this. Always act in accordance with your feelings, they will be a sure guide to the journey ahead. You will have help and happiness will result, deep and secure."

The voice had been gradually falling in pitch. Now it rose again. "Let us now answer your questions."

"But you don't know what they are."

"The cards do. And their answer is in front of me. They say patience. Show pity and kindness. You are surrounded by people who love you. And true love – a man's love – is closer than you think."

A silence fell. Kimberley thought the reading was over and was about to rise when there was a cough as the fortune teller cleared her – or his – throat.

"Beware broken promises and false friends. Be cautious. Take strength from love, for misfortune will strike. Rancour, sickness, spite, despair – others will experience these. Comfort them. Love them. Your own hopes and desires will be fulfilled in time. There will be happiness also in your household. Weddings."

"Wedding*s-s-s*? Several?"

"Yes. And babies."

Kimberley's mouth dropped open. "More than one? When will all this be?"

There was a soft chuckling. "Ah, timing! Always they want to know 'when'. Does it matter how long one must search for happiness? You must show no haste in matters that require time. Is it not enough to know that it will come? But there are signs. The Wheel of Fortune turns and returns." Some of the cards were picked up and moved a little. She hummed softly. "The tenth Major Arcana. Yes. After October. All will happen in the next six months or so. The fight will be won then, the prizes gained. Your unconscious mind knows all that I have said. I am only the instrument to bring you full awareness, to help you. Step forward now, the unknown cannot frighten you. There is a reason for everything. Create your future. Go now. Go!"

*****

Emerging from under the crimson blanket, Kimberley was reluctant to re-join the others. She felt a kind of intoxication, an expansive awareness of her surroundings, a sharpening of all her sensations and responses. Colours, sound, the fading smells of the barbecue, all crowded in on her senses as they hadn't done before.

She looked around her. Those remaining were clearing up now. Julie was still lingering by the doorway scanning for Richard.

"You don't think she meant the double yellow lines, Kim? Gipsies don't foretell bloody stupid traffic regulations, do they? I thought it was just weddings and babies. Ah, there he is," and she hurried off to ask Richard whether Wiki leaks had extended their scope.

Kimberley stood a few minutes, mulling over what she'd just heard until she saw Lisa wandering across the lawn towards her. "Do you want to see her? You're just in time if you do, but you'd better hurry."

Lisa shook her head. She looked wan.

"It could help you decide how serious Bob is. Isn't that what you want to know?"

Lisa sighed. "I know the answer to that one. He's just drifting through life, hell-bent on throwing away everything he's got that's worthwhile."

Kimberley was disturbed at the bitterness in both the words and tone of the reply. "What do you mean? Is something going on?"

Lisa looked as though she'd already regretted the outburst. "Nothing. Not that I can explain. It's just his view of life. I don't need fortune tellers to look into the future. He's going to hurt himself one day – and the people who care about him." She looked firmly down at the ground.

"And that includes you, doesn't it? You love him."

"Yes. And much good it does me." Tears were brimming in her eyes. "Maybe he appeals to the mothering instinct in me." There was a strange emphasis on the expression. "At the moment, I've just been taking the good times as they come, but I daren't look into the future. I know I won't like it, whatever it is."

She put out a hand to steady herself against the wall.

Kimberley threw her arm around her while she hunted for an appropriate response to this outpouring. "Last night must have taken it out of you, girl. Have you eaten? I don't remember seeing you have any breakfast."

"No. I wasn't feeling too good. Sick."

Kimberley started to smile sympathetically, but the look in Lisa's eyes stopped her in her tracks. A sudden realisation dawned.

"You're not… Oh, no! Bob?"

"Who else?" Lisa snapped back angrily.

The news washed over her like a tsunami. "Does he know?"

"No. I only found out when I called back home before I came here. No one else knows but you. And don't you tell him or I'll kill you. I'll tell him when the right moment comes. Not yet. I want to get used to the idea myself, first."

She wandered off without another word, and Kimberley judged the time was not right to follow her. Besides, she had to absorb the gipsy's revelations as well as the two bombshells from her friends. One wedding and one baby already. How many more?

She went to let the two dogs out; they were always shut in at first as both of them had slick (if gentle) ways of craftily detaching small children from the food they held in their chubby little hands. Virtually all the guests had gone home now. After some half-hearted enquiries, as to whether she could be of any help to anyone in the clearing up, she climbed the stairs to her bedroom – the blankets in the hall had already been removed and everything restored to its former state – shutting the door behind her quietly and going to sit on the foot of her bed. She felt excessively weary, the activities of the past twenty-four hours providing no defence against the drain of emotions she had just experienced. She tried to pick her way through the words and phrases surging through her recollections.

How could someone so accurately describe her private dilemma? And the future; the prophecy carried a hidden menace of events and disturbances that lay ahead. But there was comfort and reassurance. She would come to no harm if she trusted her feelings. Happiness will be hers, and love. The analysis of her present situation showed insight and the predictions showed authority. Hard to believe they were all due to sheer luck. Could Bob be behind this? Certainly, she acknowledged his intuitive skill in reading people. He had a keen awareness of others' troubles. It lay at odds with the catalogue of irresponsible and sometimes hurtful acts in his life.

At least, Julie's news was all good. How nice to have a best friend for a sister-in-law.

*****

Supper with the family and key helpers was a happy affair. Richard had announced the news first to Irene then the others and it bathed the proceedings in a benign glow. While it was very clear that Irene had substantial doubts about the moral suitability of a single mother as a bride for a Weatherby scion, Richard's obvious happiness and Julie's carefully contrived demeanour overrode such scruples.

However, the cheerful mood had dissipated by breakfast the following day. As soon as Kimberley joined Irene and Richard at the table, Irene began by saying, "Do you both remember that foreign-looking gentleman who arrogantly introduced himself to us at the funeral? Well, I saw him yesterday, here – walking around the lawn as though he owned the place. And when I asked him what he was doing, he had the nerve to say he was invited."

"He was. Bob invited him."

Irene paused. "I don't believe a word of it. Bob would never do that. He must have been joking and the idiot didn't realise. Anyway, I soon sent him packing."

"That could be unfortunate. Bob was trying to sell him a car. And I'm trying to sell him a flat."

"Oh, well, I'm sorry about that, but we can't tolerate gatecrashers."

"Where is Bob, anyway?" asked Kimberley.

"Gone back to uni," said Richard through a mouthful of bacon.

"Already?"

"Yes. He left yesterday. While you were closeted with Gipsy Gladys. For rather a long time, I might add."

Irene looked sharply at Kimberley. "I thought you weren't going to participate in that. You didn't believe any of that nonsense, did you? Because I prayed last night that no harm was done. I strongly disapprove of it. But as it's unlikely there'll be another employee barbecue, he can't get up to any more mischief."

"Why not?" chorused the siblings.

But Irene just shrugged and left the table, saying as she left the room, "So we won't have to put up with any unwanted guests again."

"Who were invited," muttered Kimberley under her breath. Not that she felt any need to defend the alleged interloper, but her sense of fair play and caution against Irene's domination required some kind of defence. And later that day, although she avoided any mention of the incident, she was markedly more warm and sympathetic at the viewing of a second flat. Paul responded with a bemused condescension at her new helpfulness but this flat did not meet his approval either.

"Nice but not central. And it could be a bit bigger."

"The owner might be prepared to discount the rent." They were both leaning against the lounge window sill scanning the interior while absorbing the rather dull view over Douglas rooftops.

"Not an issue. The rent is okay." He looked at her keenly. "Were you born when the business with Sir Philip split up?"

The question was a surprising diversion. Her professional skills kicked in. Why had she not noticed his attention wandering? And why this interminable appetite for the family history? Keep the customer happy, though. "Yes. Dad was married but not to Irene, Bob's mother. She's his second wife. When he divorced Shirley, his first wife and Richard's and my mother, we were quite small. As soon as they married, Irene became pregnant with Bob. In fact, I suspect she was pregnant already. There was some bad feeling between the partners' wives at the time, I believe. Still is."

"That was obvious at the funeral," mused Paul. "Why don't you work for the family business?"

The question unnerved Kimberley.

"It just sort of happened. I'd been sent away to boarding school – no, that's not quite how it was. Irene wanted us all to have a private education. Richard refused point-blank because he wanted to stay with his existing friends. He was doing well at the local school, anyway. I wasn't as bright and Irene persuaded my father that I would benefit – he wasn't bothered whatever we did as long as we were happy."

"Did you miss your family?"

"I missed my father dreadfully. He was always such fun. Bob takes after him, I think. Irene, I was never close to. I was only five when we came to live with my father and I suppose I couldn't understand why another lady had replaced my mummy. She did all the right things – I cannot fault her, but she's not a person you can take to easily." She sensed an unspoken agreement. "I think she cared about her stepchildren – still does – but it's not obvious. Not like it is with Bob."

"So was it Irene's presence in the business that deterred you?" He seemed eager to lay any blame in that quarter.

"No. She only became involved when Dad died. I just wasn't interested in cars. But I knew that I did like houses and dealing with people. Estate agency seemed the obvious choice."

"You seem to be a person who knows what she wants."

Kimberley fell silent. Was she? "I used to be," she said slowly, "but that seems like a long time ago. I'm just drifting at the moment. I feel I need some purpose in my life. I just don't know what to do."

Appalled at the revelation, she looked up at him hesitantly but he did not comment. His face had changed somehow. It was now an open book where shadows of interest and concern fell across the features. She read a hint of shyness but also strength and other gentler qualities – kindness, honesty and loyalty. Whereas his eyes' colour used to resemble a dark absorbing night, now they flashed a gleaming obsidian.

"What happened?"

Out it all came about John and the betrayal. Echoes of the good times, the happy memories, shared interests, mutual caring and then the sudden collapse of everything on which she'd built her life and her future. It was the first time she had been able to recount the story to anyone, not until now trusting herself to express the emotions she felt without degenerating into drivel, or, worse, tears. She'd only met this man a few days ago, she knew next to nothing about him, he repeatedly confused and annoyed her and yet it was to him that she'd just exposed her soul, without ever consciously deciding to do so.

A surge of embarrassment sent the blood rushing to her cheeks. She hadn't meant to say anything about John. It was so personal, banal. "I don't normally talk like this. I'm sorry." She deftly turned the conversation. "So what about you? What do you do in life? And why exactly have you come here? Or is everything a secret?"

He looked away and, for one moment, Kimberley believed she'd been too forthright. Scared him off? Not the right thing to do with a customer.

"I – um – work in IT."

"Oh." Not terribly interesting. But it might explain his interest in the Galbraith family.

"You may as well know. You mentioned that Sir Philip had a daughter. Well, she didn't go trekking in the Himalayas and get eaten by a yeti. She went to Goa before it became the youth tourist destination that it is today. There she met – and married – an Indian gentleman. She had a son, but she died ten years ago. Sir Philip was advised but all her letters and the one from the solicitor advising her death were then returned. Unopened."

"How do you know all this?" But then the realisation flashed upon her and her whole body went rigid. She had to breathe in deeply to say anything more. "Oh my god!. You're saying that all your *mother's* letters were returned?"

He nodded, and Kimberley could see her own reflection in his eyes' sombre depths, "Now I think I know who did that. The letters never reached Sir Philip."

A smattering of rain fell against the window and distracted their thoughts. A slight wind had risen, herald of more rain to come.

"So that's why you have an English name." Then the full realisation hit Kimberley. "Hell's bells! So you are an inheritor with Freddie! And as the son of the eldest child, you must precede him. Maybe the house is yours. And half the business, too!" The thought of Freddie getting his comeuppance gave her an unworthy pleasure. "What are you going to do?"

"Nothing. I don't need anything. But I did want to see my relations. And learn a bit more about the English side of the family. And, please, keep all this to yourself. I don't want anyone else to know. Not yet, anyway."

The conversation lapsed.

Kimberley sighed and, with some difficulty, switched back on her sales persona. "So you aren't interested in this flat, then?"

His smile was rueful. "I'm sorry, no."

Another hiatus. "We don't have any others of this size nearer the centre. Are you sure a small house wouldn't suit you better? There is more choice."

He reflected a few moments. "Okay. Let me see what you have."

"I'll be able to arrange at least one viewing tomorrow if you want."

Paul assented. "And maybe we could have lunch together."

This time, Kimberley found herself looking forward to the following day.

Chapter 6

Kimberley had to stay late at work that evening. When she arrived home she was surprised to find Anna hovering distraught between the kitchen and the dining room and Irene and Richard nowhere to be seen.

"They're in there." Anna pointed down the hallway to Irene's study but as Kimberly was deciding whether to break in on the meeting or amuse herself until they emerged for the evening meal, Anna burst into tears.

"What's wrong, Anna?" Kimberley turned hurriedly and threw her arms around the sobbing girl.

No answer.

Kimberley held her close for a few minutes before she asked again.

"I – I'm having a ba – baby!"

Kimberley resisted the impulse to ask who the father was. It was yet another question to which she was certain she knew the answer. She drew back a little and hunted for a safer question.

"Have you told anyone, Anna?"

"No!" she wailed. "She will send me away."

Kimberley resumed her comforting hug. "No one will send you away if you don't want to go. How far gone are you?" A sad shrug. Maybe she didn't understand the expression. "Have you seen a doctor?" A shake of the head. "What do you want to do?"

"I don't know!" she whimpered.

"Hmm. Neither do I," thought Kimberley. Aloud, with a lot more conviction than she felt: "It will all be okay. Just don't tell anyone just yet. Leave it with me, and we'll work out what to do. Just tell me one thing – do you want to keep the baby?"

Anna pulled away from her in horror. "Of course! It would be a sin!"

Damn! Kimberley had forgotten the significance of Anna's Roman Catholic background. They heard the study door open. Urging Anna to keep things secret for the moment, Kimberley felt overwhelmed by the hope and trust in the other girl's eyes. This was going to be a tricky problem to solve. *'Two babies!'* As predicted by that stupid gipsy.

The expressions on Irene's and Richard's faces did not offer much improvement in mood.

"What's wrong?" The question was becoming tediously repetitive.

Irene was fingering her jacket collar nervously. "Let's have dinner and we'll discuss it."

Once Anna had placed all the dishes on the table and disappeared back to the kitchen to attend to the custard for the plum crumble, Irene pushed her plate away.

"I must have been clairvoyant yesterday when I suggested that this barbecue could be the last."

"Don't say that," murmured Richard soothingly. "Let's see what happens first."

"It's already happened, hasn't it?" came the sharp rejoinder. "Kimberley, I had three pieces of bad news this morning. Firstly the Galbraiths confirmed that they will not be selling or leasing to us the land. And simultaneously the Indian company have advised me by email that they are not continuing the discussions with us."

"Hell's bells! Did they give any reason?"

"They implied that they didn't think that we could handle the volumes they expected. It's as though they knew about the land deal falling through."

"I suspect they did," muttered Richard as he helped himself to some vegetables. "We've been upfront about it right from the start. I guess that the same person who stopped the land deal leaked this to the Indians."

Irene covered her face with her hands. "How could she do it?"

"You think it was Lady Galbraith? Not Freddie? Or someone else, even?"

"Frederick probably would have had to make the actual decision as the heir, but it has his mother's fingerprints all over it. God may move in mysterious ways but Lady Galbraith does not."

"Wait a minute!" exclaimed Kimberley. "We don't know whether he is the heir. Sir Philip's will hasn't been published yet."

The two looked at her as though she'd just sung a rousing chorus of *Yes, we have no bananas!*

Faced with their incredulity, Kimberley realised that she could not disclose Paul's recent revelations. And, anyway, why would Sir Philip leave anything to a daughter he'd not heard from for over twenty years? She desperately wished she hadn't said anything. However, it was apparent that they thought she'd been talking nonsense and, hopefully, would instantly forget it. A quick change of subject was needed.

"You said there were three bits of bad news."

Irene sighed. "As if the first two weren't enough. Yes, Smith Greenberg, the big American bank has closed their account with us."

"And they were our biggest customer," added Richard. "When I spoke to them last month they were disputing the bill for a repair. Apparently it hadn't been satisfactory." He took another pork chop; stress never dented Richard's appetite.

"I went down to the workshop to see the manager, Kelly, to ask about it, and I got a blast of abuse. The things he called me! So I told him to apologise and watch his language in future. Then the moron handed me the wrench he was holding and walked out, saying he was quitting. With a host of unpleasant expletives."

This was bad news. Neil Kelly was Lisa's father. With a grandchild on the way – which he didn't yet know about – throwing away an income in the present tight job market was an unwise indulgence.

"So what does all this mean for the business?" asked Kimberley cautiously, pushing away the rest of her meal.

"You *are* going to eat that, Kimberley, aren't you?" warned Irene acidly.

"It means we're up shit creek without a paddle."

"Richard! Language!"

"I think you'd better light some candles and pray extra earnestly tonight, Mum. Still, miracles do happen, they say." More munching.

Kimberley felt unable to offer any more useful advice. The meal progressed in virtual silence. Only Richard's appetite did it justice. Anna dutifully served the pudding without a word, having preoccupations of her own, but she furtively threw Kimberley heartfelt pleading glances. It made continuing to participate in the family meal very uncomfortable. Kimberley was glad to escape to the television room as soon as she decently could to mull over today's bombshells.

It was while she was listlessly thumbing through the *'Radio Times'* and half-watching some mindless game show that the landline telephone rang. She did not react at first, her mind stuffed full of the revelations of the past twenty-four hours. It was probably Lisa whom she had intended to ring during the day but she did not recognise the caller ID. And anyway, Lisa would ring her mobile.

"Hello. Is that Bob Weatherby's house?" A young male voice.

"Yes."

"Who am I speaking to, please?"

"This is his sister, Kimberley. Who is this?"

"Is Bob there?"

"No, he went back to London yesterday. Why don't you try his mobile? I can give you the number if you can just hang on a minute."

"It's all right. I've got it and I've been ringing all day but he's not answering. And he's not at his flat. Can you let him know that Chris called?"

"Sure, but I'm sure you'll speak to him before I do. Bye."

Kimberley tried ringing Bob's mobile phone herself but was told that the person she was ringing was unable to take her call right now and to please try later. Much later, when she was turning off the television to go to bed, the landline telephone rang again. This time the voice was a timorous female.

"Is that Bob Weatherby's house?"

"Yes. I'm his sister. Can I help?"

"Oh, I'm sorry. I hope you don't mind me disturbing you this late, but we're worried about Bob. He wasn't in classes today. My name's Maggie, I'm a friend, and I've just come away from his flat. Some police were there, and they wanted to know where he was. I've just heard that his friend Mark's been arrested and it looks as though Bob's in some sort of trouble. I hope you don't mind me ringing you at home, I got your num–"

"Is it for me?" Irene's voice called from her study but she sounded more apprehensive than eager to talk to anyone.

Kimberley hurriedly reassured her then gave her attention to the caller.

She dropped her voice to avoid being heard. "Say that again – about the police."

"They were at the flat and wanted to talk to him."

"About what?"

"They didn't say. But I think Mark's arrest is something to do with the student union funds."

"Isn't Bob treasurer of that?"

Maggie hesitated. "Yes. I suppose it could be linked. But I don't know. And no one can get hold of him and he's not answering his mobile. Look, please don't say anything 'cos I could have got it all wrong. But if you do hear from him, please pass on the message and ask him to call me. Would you, *please*?" The voice wavered with its pleading.

"Yes. Thank you for your help. I'll try and get hold of him. Bye." Kimberley hung up then did 1471 to retrieve Maggie's number before hurrying up to Richard's room. He was fiddling about on his laptop when she entered at his invitation. It looked like a personal budget. As if he didn't have enough figures to work on during the day. The background music sounded like Mozart.

Richard listened with his usual impassive but thorough attention while she recounted the two phone calls. Kimberley waited patiently while the mind absorbed the information.

"Have you given him any money?"

"Yes. Most times he comes home he asks for some sort of loan, but I cannot remember him ever actually paying them back. Why do you ask? If he expected to get some money from me, then surely he wouldn't have any need to pinch from the Student Union coffers."

"Unless he was repaying a loan – so-called – he had from the fund. He asked me for money as well. As usual. This time I gave him £500."

Kimberley gasped. Even without anything from Irene, that was an awful lot of money he went back with.

Kimberley sat on the bed and sighed. "I've learnt quite a lot about Bob these last few days that I didn't have an inkling about before."

Richard raised a laconic eyebrow and waited for elaboration. But Kimberley decided that now was not the time to reveal her younger brother's procreative lapses.

"The Galbraith's have got their Freddie the Unsteady and now we've got Bob the Slob."

Richard looked at her aslant. "Funny you should say that. It's very weird, you know. When we were at the funeral, did you notice anything about Fred?"

"What do you mean?"

"Didn't you think he looked like Bob? Ignore Freddie's lack of hair. I was looking at him from the side and his profile was identical to that of Bob. If he had Bob's shock of curls, they could be brothers. Now they even have a similar dissolute life. Perhaps it's a curse – a pox on both our houses!"

The observation reminded Kimberley of Gipsy Gladys' predictions. Good grief! Did that woman, whoever she was, know everything? Richard's attention seemed to be exhausted as he started entering more data on his computer. Kimberley dragged her thoughts back to the latest dilemma.

"I've tried ringing him on his mobile but he won't answer. Do you think we should do anything?"

Richard shook his head. "Not yet. I don't think we have a Lord Lucan scenario here. He's obviously decided to lie low for a bit. Keep ringing and sending texts. I'll keep trying too. Sooner or later he'll make contact because he's going to need some help. And money, no doubt. Bloody idiot! Just don't say anything to Mum just yet. She's got enough to worry about with the business."

"Are things as bad as she thinks?"

He leaned over and turned up the music a smidgeon. "Let's just say, they're not good, Kimberley. Be glad you're out of it. Though if things do go belly up, we can kiss goodbye to everything. Including this house."

On an impulse, before she settled down to sleep, Kimberley rang James. Why hadn't she thought of him before?

"I just gave him a lift to the airport. No, he didn't seem any different from normal. He was anxious to get back; he said he wanted to get some revision in before the resit exams next week. I don't know of any problem. I'm too busy looking forward to our date next Saturday. What kind of meal do you like?"

But Kimberley wasn't in the mood to discuss fripperies. She'd been careful not to mention the student union fund situation. How serious was that? It seemed unlikely. So after a few desultory remarks, she pleaded tiredness and rang off.

A grey mood settled on her. So many of the people she loved were troubled yet paradoxically, she herself felt quite safe, as though a shield separated her from their sorrows and grief. A sudden shock skittered through her body. Why was, that thought familiar? Where had she heard that idea recently? She began to laugh when she realised that it had been Gipsy Gladys but then ceased. Other parts of that encounter came back into her mind but the sequence of thoughts was confused.

In the beginning she had been identified with the Queen of Swords, signifying change, progress and conflict. She was stunned at the exact parallel of her present situation, but the reading had foretold not only upheaval and disturbing events in the near future, but advised patience which would result in happiness – but later. Why not now? Wasn't the sequence of events moving faster?

What else had the Gipsy said? Kimberley was now concerned that she could not remember clearly. Only scattered phrases came to mind. Something about trusting, comforting others, acting in accordance with her feelings. Oh, yes, and that strange remark, "True love is closer than you think."

The whole realisation gave rise to a certain unease. Who had the right to foretell her future? She remembered Irene's warning – and then the Gipsy's message of reassurance. No, no harm would come to her, she had promised. And there was nothing sinister in Gipsy Gladys, whoever she was. Maybe she could simply take advice and comfort from the predictions; to trust, to console, to wait, then let life take whatever course it must. But now, she carefully stored these thoughts away, to be recalled if needed as the next few months unfurled before her.

Chapter 7

The following week was full of incident. After a satisfactory Tuesday catching up with some personal chores and shopping for a new dress for Saturday's hot date, Kimberley had a surprisingly pleasant lunch the next day with the inscrutable Mr Panesar. *And* he immediately decided to buy the house he had just viewed. Now that she knew who he was, they could converse freely, although Kimberley later decided that she had been too unguarded when catching up with family gossip. But nothing was said about Bob, even though Kimberley suspected her brother would claim an introductory share of the sales commission. She was airily vague when Paul asked about him and was relieved that he had the tact not to pursue it.

Unusually, she heard nothing from Lisa but then, the family was probably adjusting to the main breadwinner walking out of his job in a strop. Meanwhile at home Anna threw alternately pleading and conspiratorial looks across at her for which Kimberley had no suitable response. She had to resort to reassuring nods and once even a wink, for heaven's sake.

Friday brought the stunning news that Braithby Business Solutions had been taken over by an Indian software company. Kimberley wondered whether there was any connection with Paul but decided it was merely a coincidence. Widespread speculation followed about the future roles of Freddie and his mother but a press release explaining everything was not due until the following week. Meantime, Freddie was believed to be cavorting around Mayfair with his drugged-up floozies as usual.

Overshadowing everything was the situation with Bob, of course. Kimberley rang his mobile every hour or so – as did Richard – but he remained resolutely unobtainable. It was on Saturday that things started to boil up.

Kimberley got a brief and unexpected telephone call from Richard when she was out with a client. She was unable to discuss anything at the time, and her brother's news that the police had just called at Prospect House begged examination. Even the thought of Irene's undoubted berating of the unfortunate police officers tasked with the visit did not offer her any amusement. As soon as she could, she sent Bob an urgent text and was gratified when she at last got a phone call from him at the office during the afternoon.

"I can't talk long." His voice sounded muffled.

"Where are you?"

"I'm just lying low for a bit. Don't worry. Just leave me in peace while I get some things sorted."

Kimberley began in a low key. "Some friends of yours, Chris and Maggie phoned here. Good job Irene didn't answer the calls. They said you hadn't been to any lectures. And what about those exam resits?"

He cleared his throat rather noisily. "It's useless. Old Chapman, the economics guy – or gay, should I say – has now actually come right out and *propositioned* me – as I think the correct term is. Otherwise I won't pass."

"What do you mean?" But Bob declined to elaborate so Kimberley pushed on to more contentious matters. "They said the police had been snooping round your flat and someone, a friend, had been arrested. They even called at the house here this morning. It's something to do with the student union –"

But Bob interrupted her. "Look, it's all just a misunderstanding, an accounting error. They're all a bunch of idiots, anyway."

"And what about Anna?"

"What *about* Anna?"

"She's pregnant."

There was an uncharacteristic pause before he answered, "So?"

"Well, what are you going to do about it? The poor girl's frantic."

"Nothing. Not my problem."

"Of course, it's your problem. It's your baby!"

"Who says? She could be lying. Who knows who the little slut's been sleeping with?"

"Bob, you know that's not the case. She never goes out anyway, and she adores you. Abandoning her is just immoral."

Bob gave a harsh, cynical laugh. "Immoral! Don't talk to me about morality. That's a mug's charter – people just kick you in the teeth regardless."

Kimberley frantically considered what strategy to use to make plain the seriousness of the situation. "Irene doesn't know about it yet but sooner or later, she –"

"Get off my fucking back, will you?"

Kimberley almost dropped her phone with shock. But when she tried to remonstrate with him, he'd rung off.

The rest of the afternoon passed in a blur. The nasty reality was that Bob's lackadaisical approach to life had severe limitations and not those that Kimberley could easily accept. She invented an excuse to leave work promptly, something about her stepmother having a freak accident with a butter curler or whatever.

Richard was not at home when she arrived. Must be with Julie. Before risking any encounter with Irene, she rang him to discuss tactics. When she revealed the news about the two prospective grandchildren, she was deeply irritated that he did not consider the situation of any great concern.

"It happens," was his laconic observation, oblivious to any trauma to the abandoned girls.

"But he has responsibilities to both of them."

"Kim, it takes two to tango. If they didn't take precautions, it's just as much their fault as his. We're not in the Middle Ages, you know."

Men! "So I'm just being stupid to be so upset?"

"Yes, you are, rather." Missing the irony.

But he did agree that Irene should be told and the sooner, the better. Kimberley was further annoyed to realise that that duty now rested squarely with her. And she was due to be collected by James within three-quarters of an hour for the promised meal.

"Ah, well," she thought, *"once again, a woman has to step up to the plate."*

She hastily showered and dressed before going in search of her stepmother. Irene was in the lounge holding some precious *objets d'art* and checking whether Anna had dusted along the shelves. How to broach the matter?

"Have you heard from Bob since he went back to London?"

Irene checked her finger for dust. "No, he's usually too busy working to ring. No news is good news. Although I am a bit worried about those police calling."

"Did they say what it was about?"

"I didn't give them chance. They must have got the wrong person, anyway. Bob would never do anything stupid, let alone criminal." She gave a controlled but awkward laugh.

"He rang me this afternoon." Irene looked at her sharply. "He is in some trouble. It seems some money's gone missing –" Irene stopped her dust inspection and started fiddling with one of her earrings – "and so has he. He insists it's all a misunderstanding –"

"Of course it is," Irene asserted, but her expression had changed to one of nervous apprehension.

"That's as may be. But I think you should also know that both Lisa and Anna are pregnant by him."

Irene grabbed the arm of the sofa and sat down abruptly. It took only a moment before she had rationalised the situation and regained command of herself. "That's just nonsense. My son does not consort with harlots. They're obviously trollops. They're trying to pin the blame on Bob because he's rich so they can squeeze some money out of him. And he's so good-natured that he might take pity on them and help. I shall have to put a stop to this."

Kimberley was astounded at the denial. Family loyalty was one thing; wilful blindness to reality was quite another. She wondered whether she should argue the case but was mindful that James was due in twenty minutes, and she still had to put her face on. Oh, so what the hell!

"For God's sake, why do you keep defending Bob? Can't you see how foolish that makes you look? He's not perfect. He doesn't fly around the world in a cape with his underpants over his trousers. He's human, like the rest of us. Your persistent indulgence can only make him worse."

She might have been haranguing a kitchen roll. A fixed icy expression fastened itself onto Irene's face. She stood up abruptly. *"Mine enemies would daily swallow me up: for they be many that fight against me,"* she muttered to herself. "Family *matters*, Kimberley. Anyone else has to take second place. Anna will have to go. Is she still in the kitchen, do you know? She always did waste food, anyway."

Kimberley grabbed hold of her arm, as she passed, "No! Don't you dare speak to Anna yet! Why not find out whether it is Bob's baby first?"

Irene looked fiercely scornful, "People do bear false witness, Kimberley. It's not just a biblical myth. Don't be fooled by Anna's Roman Catholic protestations. She's just as scheming as every foreigner here is. Always looking out for themselves."

"You're not going to fire Anna! She doesn't know what she's going to do yet. She's terribly worried and doesn't have anywhere to go. We've got to help her. And she's carrying your grandchild!"

"I very much doubt that's the case. And if she's worried now, she should have thought more carefully before opening her legs to all and sundry." She swept out, followed by an agitated Kimberley who extended her hold to both arms as they both made a clumsy progress towards the kitchen. Anna

95

was preparing the evening meal. When they reached the door, she smiled fleetingly at Kimberley but swiftly changed her expression to fear when she saw Irene's harsh look matched to her tone.

"Anna, we need to talk. I hear –" As Kimberley tried to shuffle into the kitchen with her, Irene slammed the door shut behind her, trapping her wrists. Kimberley drew back from the pain and Irene completed the action, leaning against the door to prevent Kimberley pushing it open and entering. The door was solid, so apart from hearing voices, she could not make out the words. As she rubbed her badly bruised wrists, she soon heard Anna's plaintive wail then sobs.

"Oh, my God, surely she's not firing her," thought Kimberley, never doubting Irene's rigid, unwavering resolve. She felt tears welling up herself but screwed her eyes shut then went upstairs. The damage was done. There was little she could do to help right now and James was due in ten minutes. Damn Irene! Damn her to hell! She'd never admitted to such feelings before.

*****

"Are you okay?" James asked after they'd ordered their meal at the smart seafood restaurant by the harbour.

No, she wasn't, but she hesitated before admitting it. The last thing she wanted to do was reveal her family's dirty secrets to outsiders.

"Just a headache. It's been a busy week."

"Does that mean lots of houses sold? Lots of money?"

"None of your business," she found herself thinking but her answer was more diplomatic. "A few good prospects," she smiled feebly. "How about you?"

"Business is good, as usual. But I leave all that to Dad."

"Are your parents back home now?"

"Yes, but they're out tonight at some sort of business do."

"Why didn't you go?"

He smiled conspiratorially. "I explained that I had a prior engagement. One that I very much didn't want to miss."

Strangely, Kimberley remained unimpressed. It all sounded so clichéd, as though he'd rehearsed it a thousand times. Or maybe recent events had left her much more cynical than before. As the meal progressed, her preoccupation with recent events persisted while James, to his credit, tried multiple topics to engage his companion in conversation, ranging from the weather, international politics, local business prospects and the Manx space industry, which Kimberley admittedly did find of interest. He even cracked a couple of jokes – of dubious provenance, given the occasion. The sort you find on Penguin biscuit wrappers. Eventually, compassion overcame her anxieties. What girl is not flattered, when her escort tries the whole gamut of tricks to reach out, amuse and comfort her. Simply the effort was heart-winning.

"Look, James, I'm sorry. I've been looking forward to this for a week but – how can I explain? – I'm just too worried about a lot of things at the moment, especially Bob."

"I heard from him yesterday."

"Really? What did he say?"

"Nothing much. But he sounded fine. Just fine." James' expression indicated that there was nothing more to discuss and disrupt the evening.

Should she tell him what she knew? No, not yet. Not enough trust there. An awkward silence resumed.

James' expression softened as he stretched out his hand to cover hers. "Kimberley, you're looking troubled. Do you want to tell me what's worrying you?"

An inner sense cautioned her. She shook her head and returned his gaze with appropriate regret. "Family matters. I – I can't say anything. It'll pass. These things do. I'm just finding it difficult to find the energy to concentrate on the present."

His eyes seemed to penetrate her soul. "The world's energy flows into us and through us. It emanates from the very centre of your being. You must be at one with the world. Everything you think and do is a vibrant part of the song of life."

Her astonishment must have been overt. He withdrew his hand and shifted in his chair.

"I've studied Sufism a bit," he mumbled. "Diane's into things like that. Kimberley, you look as though you could do with a holiday."

"Well, I have one planned. It's too busy during the summer, so I'm taking two weeks at the beginning of November, going to Tenerife with my friend Lisa." This wasn't looking too certain right now.

"I'm going to Turkey next week, driving across Europe in the car. I'm doing a bit of business, but that won't take up much time. How about getting some time off and coming with me? Just the two of us?"

His intense smile indicated some activities to pass the time that even her own brother wouldn't have suggested.

After the momentary surprise, Kimberley did not find the invitation as attractive as she would have expected.

"In the BMW?"

"Of course. Fast and comfortable."

"Exactly how much discount did Bob get you on that?"

James smiled cryptically.

"A lady doesn't ask that sort of question of a man," he murmured.

Kimberley stiffened as an arrow of resentment streaked through her. Just how close was this guy's friendship with her wayward brother? Enough to baulk a seduction of his sister? She pushed around on her plate the remains of a pear *tarte tatin*, her appetite rapidly vanishing.

He reached across the table and placed his hand on hers, "You don't have to decide right now. Sleep on it. Better still, come home with me, Kimberley. Let's finish the evening together, just the two of us."

"Diane's not at home?"

"No, she's out with her friends celebrating. It was her birthday yesterday."

Kimberley gazed into those gorgeous brown eyes, honey-sweet with intense yearning. The offer was tempting. What was the alternative? Irene would almost certainly still be up if she went home now. She smiled as warmly as she could manage and nodded.

As they drove, the mood lightened. James obviously considered the wooing was reaching a successful conclusion. Kimberley relished the adventure and the reassurance of her continuing allure. She felt entitled to some excitement.

The house echoed slightly as they entered the heavy front door. She was foolishly expecting to be shown into the lounge; with a start, she saw James indicating that she should climb the imposing stairway in front of them. Brushing her misgivings aside, they went up side by side. The landing area was generous and, as they passed along towards the scene of intended seduction, she saw through an open door what must be Diane's bedroom. A faint but familiar perfume emanated from the room. Birthday cards littered all the surfaces and an assortment of clothes and books were strewn over a showily oversized bed. To her astonishment, there was a large, garish poster – a naked male with a long beard, antlers, and a horse-like tail prancing sideways with the words 'The Sorcerer' below. Then the title of one of the books, a large volume, caught her sharp eye, making her stop in her tracks: 'Witchcraft Today'. After a moment's hesitation, she entered the room and picked it up to examine it.

"Is Diane a witch?" she asked after a quick perusal. The question seemed shocking – or ridiculous.

"I don't think so, but magic has always interested her."

A realisation dawned. "She was Gipsy Gladys, wasn't she?"

James shrugged. "All I know is that she predicted I would get my heart's desire this week." Whether true or not, there was no mistaking the effect he intended.

"If you're trying to seduce me…" The ambiguous ending hung in the air between them. James raised his eyebrows a fraction, and his smile deepened as though relishing the thought.

So the predictions were all rubbish. The weddings and babies were just egregious coincidences. She could dismiss them from her mind entirely. And yet… Raising the devil may be mere chicanery but the agent is answerable for any ensuing mischief, for sure. Kimberley replaced the book thoughtfully. He moved his hand to the small of her back and steered her gently into his bedroom. She liked how it felt and she began to think how his hands would feel spreading over her body.

It was a good night. No, it was a *wonderful* night. Passionate, fulfilling, healing, marvellous, a wonderful night.

Chapter 8

"Get rid of it?"

The news shot out of her mind all thoughts of James and the emotional parting earlier that morning. She stared in horror and dismay at her friend.

Lisa's usual snugly warmth had been replaced by an icy resolve. She was sitting calmly and rigidly on the worn family sofa. Intensive TV advertising of perpetual credit and improbably slashed prices had left this household unmoved.

"Yes." The answer was considered and final.

"But you love babies! And Bob. Don't you?"

There was a brief pause. "I don't want anything more to do with the Weatherby family. They're arrogant, self-serving and vicious."

"Including me?" Kimberley was thunderstruck.

"Including anyone who follows that matriarch bitch's lead."

"But I don't. You know I don't. Why, I don't even work for the family business!"

"Or even who seeks her approval for a suitable dress at corporate events."

That stung. "Does it include Julie?"

"Yes. It seems even she now kowtows to Irene. That woman is all steel. All her victims are willing, feeding her demons. She scares them to death, drawing their strength from them. No one can reach any feelings she may have."

Kimberley sat stunned at the spite, "You're crazy! You're giving up your friends, cutting off your nose to spite your face. And Bob doesn't even know about the baby yet. Or does he?"

Lisa shook her head. "And he never will. Unless you betray me."

"No. You know I wouldn't." Not after the last fiasco with Anna, she wouldn't. Kimberley fidgeted with the shoulder strap of her handbag while she considered the new information. "Do you know a doctor who will help you?"

"That's my business."

Another pause.

"At the risk of sounding trite, do I assume that you won't be coming on our Tenerife holiday as planned? Because the rest of the money has to be paid now."

Lisa nodded wryly. "That's a loss I'll have to take."

They sat in a prickly silence. Kimberley sensed the meeting was at an end. She got up to leave then hesitated, looking at Lisa. "What are you going to do now then? Just carry on as before?"

"I've been thinking very hard about my future during the last few days. I've decided that I'm going to train as a nurse."

"Leave the island?"

"Yes. I've applied to a London teaching hospital. A completely new start. Maybe my life will amount to something then. And help Mum and Dad."

Kimberley was left speechless. The drastic change in her friend – former friend? – was astounding. There seemed nothing else to say.

"Well, as an arrogant, self-serving, vicious family member, let me wish you luck, anyway. When will you be leaving?"

"Soon, I hope. It's a late application and they may not agree, or I may have to wait a few months. Still, that's not your concern, is it? Being born rich means you don't have to worry about things like that."

She let the jibe pass. A sudden thought struck Kimberley. "How are you going to pay for all this?"

"I'll manage. Student loans and part-time jobs. I'm not afraid of hard work. And when you've cleared up as much vomit and urine as I have, you're not even terribly bothered what you do."

"Let me help! Please, Lisa. I can afford it. Maybe my family owes you this at least."

A faint nod. "Thanks, but no thanks. I don't want anything from the Weatherbys. But at least with you, I know the offer's genuine. No, I've got it all worked out."

Kimberley sighed and turned to leave once more. "I suppose all that's left to say is 'Good Luck', then. I wish you well. And if you change your mind about being friends, do *please* get in touch. Please, Lisa."

Lisa looked away as though unwilling to concede any gesture of loyalty or affection while Kimberley left the room and showed herself out of the house. As she drove home, reflecting on this latest development, not entirely convinced of Lisa's rejection of all things Weatherby, she assessed the situation. Now she had promised not to tell Bob about the baby, her options were limited. Bob could persuade anyone to do anything. Lisa's decision to terminate the pregnancy and leave to become a nurse might have been the same, but at least the friendship would have survived. The thought of a few days in Turkey, away from all this suddenly appeared very enticing.

She was pulling into the driveway at home resolving to ring James and accept the invitation when her mobile rang. It was Paul. His voice was formal but warm.

"We are due to meet this week to confirm the details of what is included in the house purchase price but I have to go back to India. My father is very ill and I want to arrange some business affairs while I'm there."

"Oh, I'm so sorry. Perhaps we can arrange it for when you come back." For some reason, she hesitated. "You are coming back?"

"Of course. Now, I remember seeing you looking in a travel agent's at an advertisement for holidays in India and I wondered whether you would like to come with me. As my guest. No obligation and no sinister motive on my part! Have you been to India before?"

"N-no. The furthest east I've been is Cyprus."

"You'll love it. And I'd love to show you the real India. Not just the tourist bits. Although I shall have to spend some time on other things, I'll make sure you are looked after. While you're deciding, would you like to have dinner with me tonight?"

Now, this was a rum do. Despite persisting warmth towards her lover of the previous night, Kimberley could not suppress a curiosity about this latest invitation. There must be a lucky conjunction in her stars just now.

"I'd love to. Come out for a meal, that is. Not sure about the travel."

"Think about it. When shall I come and pick you up?"

"No, don't go to any trouble, let me drive in and meet you somewhere."

"Okay. Is there a special restaurant you'd like to go to?"

Kimberley had a wicked thought. "Yes. How about the Tanroagan?" No matter if the staff recognised her from being there with another man last night. Let them think what they wanted about her. She could objectively compare the experience with two different escorts. "It's a seafood restaurant down by the harbour. I'll pick you up outside your hotel in an hour."

She hurried inside to get ready. Out of habit, she went to the kitchen to tell Anna not to include her for the evening meal but Anna was nowhere to be found. A sick feeling replaced her excitement for the evening to come. Fearing the worst, she went to Irene's study to find out exactly what had happened but paused outside the door – it was always kept closed – when she heard animated voices inside. One of which was that of a man.

She knocked politely and opened the door. Sitting relaxed in the easy-chair opposite Irene's desk was George Quirke. Irene glanced over at her, visibly annoyed at the interruption.

"Yes? You are disturbing an important meeting."

Kimberley had planned not so much a challenge as a declaration of war by demanding to know Anna's fate. But both her inclination and her business instinct barred her from washing the family's dirty linen in public.

"I'm dining out tonight, so I don't require an evening meal."

Irene acknowledged the information with a discreet nod but made no comment.

Kimberley withdrew quietly, shutting the door behind her. What meeting with George Quirke could be important? As she went to get ready, it occurred to her that there was perhaps a way she could help her erstwhile best friend. The randy Mr Quirke, he who couldn't keep it in his trousers, was the son of a distinguished London surgeon, now retired. Family knowledge of the medical world had prompted George to set up the investment fund specialising in health-related businesses. Maybe that knowledge and the connections also meant he could pull a few strings. Encouraged by the possibility, she hesitated before climbing the stairs.

At that moment, Irene emerged from the study and hurried past her, apparently to collect something. Kimberley re-entered the study and faced a glowing leer from its occupant.

"And how's my favourite Weatherby? Come over here," as he beckoned her with pink, chubby fingers. She noticed with distaste that the nails were dirty and chewed.

Kimberly forced a smile. "George, it's nice to see you again. I was wondering if you could help me."

His face lit up. She guessed that it was not with delight at the prospect of helping a friend but with the chance of winning an obligation from an attractive young lady which he could turn to his advantage.

She explained Lisa's career situation, omitting the pregnancy complications. They were being taken care of. As she did so, George rose and extended his arm around her waist until he was near enough so she could smell his alcohol-laden breath. She repressed the shudders.

"Of course," he re-joined. "No problem. I'll ask my father to arrange to get her accepted at the hospital she wants and check out any grants or scholarships available. Don't worry, it will all be very discreet. She'll never know. And I'm sure you can find a way to thank me later." He winked grotesquely and tightened his grip around her. It was a relief to hear Irene's high heels tapping back along the hall. He let her go with what he obviously thought was an enticing smile and sat down again in the chair.

Irene was both surprised and disapproving to find her step-daughter still in the study. Recognising the facial reprimand, Kimberley left once more and hurried to prepare for the evening's date, wondering what the pair's conference was about.

****

Like a cat on a hot summer afternoon, Kimberley stretched out in her bed later that night. No matter that it was a chilly night in late autumn, she felt as warm and languid as the doziest sun-strafed feline. She savoured again the highs, at the start and end of the day – having two gorgeous men chasing her was an overdue and refreshing change – and reflected on the disturbing meat in the day's sexual sandwich. Not that she and Paul had engaged in anything like that, goodness no! But wasn't there a tacit invitation in the thoughtful attentiveness? In those dark, smiling eyes? Promising who-knows-what.

The restaurant didn't open on Sundays, so there hadn't been a problem with the curious eyes of the waiting staff. They had simply eaten at the hotel and, no, Paul had not suggested she retired with him to his room. But the thought certainly jumped into her mind. How strange that she was now eager for his company. She could not remember what she had originally found so unpleasant about him.

Eventually she was slipping into that delicious descent towards the arms of Morpheus when she was suddenly roused. She listened. There were no strange sounds that might have disturbed the quietness. Then it occurred to her that without Anna to do it, the dogs, may not have been let out. She grabbed her robe and pattered downstairs to perform the precautionary task. There must be no puddles or smelly parcels to exacerbate Irene's mood in the morning. Mondays were full of dull routine anyway. She did not want wrath added to the mix.

There were three dogs – two sisters from an acquaintance's litter of golden retrievers and a young male, the son of one of them that Bob and Kimberley had lobbied vigorously to keep because he had such gorgeous soft ears. It was curious that none of them jumped up to greet her as she went to the scullery where they slept. It was more than curious, it was –

She switched on the light. All three dogs lay inert in their baskets. Kimberley bent down in horror to check they were breathing. She was aware of a movement behind her and turned to see what it was.

"Is that you, Richard?"

She remembered no more until she woke with a splitting headache a little while later. There was a sensation of pins and needles in her arm where she'd lain on it awkwardly but otherwise she felt okay, just that headache. She was less sanguine when she realised that the scullery door was not only closed but wedged shut from the other side. She pulled and pushed at it vainly then shouted. A few moments later she heard Richard's answering call. He located and then freed her.

"What have you been doing?" he queried.

"I was shut in here," she panted. "There must have been an intruder. And there's something wrong with the dogs. Look! It's as though they've been drugged."

Richard's fleeting glance indicated agreement at the conclusion. "Where's Mum? And what's wrong with your head?"

"I'm okay, just a bump. Irene's in her room, I suppose. She probably wouldn't have heard me on that side of the house. Suppose whoever it is, is still here?" Kimberley grabbed hold of his arm for reassurance.

"I'll check. Stay here for now while I search the ground floor. Then go and tell Mum. And I'll check if anything's been taken." He hurried off.

"Be careful!"

Seldom had she felt such gratitude to her elder brother. His sparse enthusiasm was usually directed to the deferred tax equalisation account. Or, on a good day, a new design of paperclip. Now his applied common sense and thorough investigative technique were just what was required. She turned her attention back to the dogs but speaking to them and caressing their heads brought only a limited response. Someone who knew what they were doing must have given them a powerful sedative.

Richard returned. "The French doors seem to have been forced. Why didn't Mum set the alarm? Can't tell if anything's been taken. I'll go check upstairs. I'll call if it's okay then you can wake Mum."

Some time later Kimberley was calling softly outside Irene's door but there was no answer. Richard joined her.

"Can't see anyone – or anything missing. Better go in. She'd never forgive us if we didn't tell her at once." He didn't need to add that she might not be okay.

She opened the door and stepped into the room. As she approached the bed, Irene started and hastily reached to switch on the bedside light. In the sudden blast of illumination, they could see that she was lying in the arms of George Quirke.

Chapter 9

"Let he who is without sin cast the first stone."

Irene's rejoinder had echoed repeatedly in her mind since her arrival in Bangalore. Trust her stepmother to pick the one defence of Bob's conduct for which Kimberley had no counter. Nor anyone else for that matter. Her frustration – anger, even – was now being swamped by the excitement of new sights, sounds and smells.

They had arrived at Bangalore in the morning. A sleek Mercedes car met them at the airport. "Here is Kunal, one of our drivers, and he will look after you," Paul had assured her as they got in. Before Kimberley had time to absorb her surroundings, Paul was dropped at the hospital to visit his sick father.

Kunal was nice. He spoke perfect English (as everyone seemed to), addressed her respectfully as "Ma'am", and flashed a smile a mile wide with perfect, sparkling teeth. His brief was to show her something of Bangalore during the morning until they went to Paul's family home at lunchtime, where she was to stay, and not in a hotel. Kimberley would have liked to go somewhere to freshen up first but did not plead her case as Paul was so anxious to check on his father's condition.

First of all, she was taken to Saint Mark's Cathedral. This sounded promising, despite her grubby weariness. Cool and clean, its architecture reflected a history of European influence in the country. Yes, it was pleasing to the eye but Kimberley found it hard to be impressed. Barely two hundred years old, it lacked the soaring grandeur of those cathedrals built by the Normans in north-west Europe nearly a thousand years ago. Maybe she would have found the local Indian temples more impressive. She must make sure they were included in the itinerary for another time.

Now she was making polite noises again as they walked around some botanical gardens. They were a welcome oasis in the clamorous bustle of the city but, hell's bells, there weren't many actual *flowers*. Litter, yes but few blooms. She thought of home, the modest floral displays on seaside promenades and the cool, shady glens back on the island. It prompted the reflection that maybe, as in life, continuous sunshine did not guarantee the best plant displays. You needed a lot of rain as well. And there had been too much of that for the Weatherby family lately. Much too much. Overall, she was a bit disappointed with her first experiences in India. And the day was getting uncomfortably hot. She was starting to feel drowsy. Some lunch in a cool place would be a good idea.

As they drove back to the hospital to collect Paul, Kimberley tried a little discreet questioning of Kunal about his employers. "So you work for Mr Panesar's company?"

"Oh, no, Ma'am. For the family. I worked for the company many years ago but was promoted. Now just the family. Three of us."

"The family has three chauffeurs?"

That big, bright smile again. "Yes, very busy all the time."

"And what is the family like to work for? Are they nice?"

Kunal was commendably diplomatic. "Very nice. To all of us. Mr Panesar is very kind. And Mr Paul." Another big smile.

Doubtful that she would learn anything of great insight or even novelty, she then changed tack with her interrogation. She was regaled with amusing details of Kunal's own large extended family while they drove to the Panesar family home after collecting Paul from the hospital.

If Kimberley had suffered pangs of disappointment up till now, they vanished abruptly. The partially hidden entrance gave little indication of the splendour that it concealed. A driveway slinked carefully through ornamental trees, ferns and vibrant flowers, tended vigorously by a team of perspiring gardeners. The huge expense of the lawn looked as thick and springy as a costly green carpet. Beyond this colourful expanse rose a long, porticoed façade in smooth, pinkish-white stone, graced with elegant fenestration. Not quite the Taj Mahal but what it lacked in grandeur, it made up for in graceful hospitality. It gleamed under a sun that here radiated glowing benisons as opposed to the glaring heat in the city centre. Only money, and lots of it, could buy such serenity so close to a bustling, populous, modern city.

The car drew up at a shallow flight of steps. She saw a clutch of people come out of the tall, double doors at the top as Paul took her hand to lead her up to them. She wanted to bring her luggage but noticed a man and a woman, both in smart Indian dress, hurry down, to take all the bags out of the boot and follow her.

"Take them to the second guest suite," said Paul.

"The 'second' suite? Not the first?"

"It's a bit smaller, but the views are better."

Reassured about her importance, she followed Paul through the house. Kimberley was accustomed to the trappings of a relatively wealthy home, as well as being acutely aware of the market value of luxury, but these surroundings were unambiguously impressive. Wide corridors on either side gave tantalising vistas of spacious, airy rooms full of polished wood, fine silk draperies and elegant furniture cunningly placed to elicit admiration.

"Rather too showy for my taste," she thought, *"but it would be an absolute joy to sell."*

They entered a large, shady room that had two sides open to the garden. More trees, shrubs and strange flowers encircled a brilliant green lawn. In the distance, the towers and rooves of Bangalore gleamed in the afternoon sun, and a low hum reminded visitors of the city traffic beyond the closer noise of busy insects.

A wide table set in the middle of the room was covered with fragrant cold dishes of bread, pancakes, vegetables and little pots of sauces. Two Indian men in dark silk tunics and trousers stood at one side.

"You'll be pleased that we're eating western-style."

"What does that mean?"

"Plates and knives and forks. Indian-style is on a banana leaf with fingers. You'll have a chance to try it later."

He guided her through the dishes. No meat but she was surprised not to miss it with delicious rice, vegetables and a galaxy of spicy chutneys.

Once her appetite was somewhat appeased, the conversation started.

"So you're rich, then?" She felt a bit like Elizabeth Bennet when she visited Pemberley.

115

Paul raised his eyebrows at the unabashed directness of the question, "You've never been interested enough in me to ask about my financial situation, not even when you were trying to sell me a flat. My grandfather was a Maharajah. He built this house. My father was his second son and not expecting to inherit, so I had quite an ordinary upbringing. No glamour. I expected to have to earn my living. So they packed me off to get a master's degree in IT at Imperial College in London."

"So, you're clever as well?"

Paul gave an embarrassed nod. "Maybe it runs in the family. And it was a very fashionable subject at that time in India. Still is. Anyway, my uncle never married and had any children, despite the usual family pressures."

"Was he gay?"

Paul managed to look both sheepish and affronted. "Sons of Maharajas are not gay," he iterated solemnly.

"Which means he was," thought Kimberley.

"Then he was killed, in a car accident. By this time, the government had abolished all the official titles and privileges of princes – that was in 1971, a few years before I was born. So I shall never get the twenty-one-gun salute that my grandfather was entitled to. I miss it so much…"

"So what do you do? Apart from wishing every car backfiring was in your honour?"

Were the two serving guys smiling? The fact that she noticed them must have been what prompted Paul to dismiss them with a wave. They'd been as useful as a Dutch Mountain Rescue Team anyway.

"I earn my living in computing. We have a large group of software companies. In fact we have just bought another one. In the Isle of Man."

"So it's *you* that's bought BBS!"

They were silent for a few minutes as Kimberley absorbed the news. "Do the Galbraiths know who you are? What's happened to Freddie's and Lady Galbraith's shares? Do they still have any control? Who's going to run it? Will it move to India?"

Paul held up his hand in mock protection against the torrent of questions. "Nothing will change for now. It will take some time to go through, that's what I hope to discuss with my father. Fortunately, it now looks as though he will recover. I shall need to spend some time on the Island, for the next few months while we check out a few things. The opportunities aren't going to go away. We have time, and you will learn that the Indian people are famously patient. So, if you wish, you're going to see a lot more of me. Though I don't expect to be buying any more houses."

The prospect was not unattractive. She looked around the table to see if she wanted anything more to eat.

"Have you finished?"

"I think so. But there is so much food left over."

"Don't worry about that. The servants will eat it."

"So they live on your left-overs?" At least Irene would approve.

Paul smiled wryly but did not think the remark worthy of an answer. The thought of Irene returned her attention to the unresolved problems she had temporarily escaped. She wondered if anything new happened since she'd left.

"You like Bob, don't you, Paul?"

"Why do you ask?"

"But you do, don't you?"

"Yes. He's a very likeable guy. You can tell that by the way people – even strangers – respond to him. He's been blessed with many shining qualities. Unfortunately, he demands permanent, eventless sunshine because he cannot handle anything serious or discouraging. He lacks wisdom."

It sounded a bit pompous. "Hmm. Maybe it's not wisdom that he lacks, but principles."

No one spoke for a few moments.

"He's in some kind of trouble, isn't he? You haven't talked about him recently."

Kimberley decided not to mention the pregnancies. The two girls' decisions meant they were unlikely to figure in Bob's future, anyway. However, she doubted that the suspected embezzlement was any less alienating.

"The police are after him. It seems to be something to do with student union funds."

Paul frowned. "Surely he has enough money. Doesn't he have an allowance?"

"Oh, yes, a generous one. I don't know exactly how much but I didn't go short before I was earning, so it must be more than adequate. Irene is careful about money, but she's not that mean. Or spiteful. And Bob is the favourite. I suppose it's because he's her only child. She thinks he's a saint and won't hear a word spoken against him."

"No, she doesn't think that."

Now, this was a perverse and unfounded observation. In response to the look of amazement on Kimberley's face, Paul continued. "She's hard and sharp and doesn't miss a thing, but she knows exactly what Bob's like. But she requires total control of a situation and denies anything that compromises that control. Bob is too much of a free spirit for her. So she pretends he is just what she wants him to be. Anyway, student unions don't usually have great amounts of money, so it seems unlikely that it's anything serious. Why doesn't he just admit any failing and pay up? Or get his mother to."

Kimberley pondered the logic. "I'm not sure that may be possible right now. The family business is having some difficulty." She explained about the thwarted expansion.

Paul did not spend much time considering the problems. "I can solve all this easily. As soon as things are sorted here, we'll go to Mumbai, and I'll see the motor company – they have their head office there. I'll sort everything out. And I'll check out the bit of land and sell or lease it to Weatherby's."

"But that will mean declaring who you are and claiming your inheritance. Are you sure that's what you want to do? It's one of those things that when done, cannot be undone."

As he was looking at her reflecting on her remark, she gave an enormous yawn. He slid his hand across the table to rest lightly on hers. It was a simple gesture of reassurance but the effect was electric. As if a blinding blue flash emitted from the firm but gentle contact. Just as though electric circuitry had replaced bone and sinew. She looked into his eyes to interpret his intention but could only identify a luminous solicitude bouncing straight back at her. It was impossible to read what was going on in his mind. His face gave no clue. But his voice was soft and tender.

"You must be very tired. Let me show you to your suite and you can rest this afternoon while I see our lawyers. Or you can wander about the house and garden if you prefer. I'll find you when I return. Then we can see downtown Bangalore and have dinner. We can go to the Love Shack if you want. It's a nightclub with karaoke. But it has to close by 11.30. Sharp. The police are very hot on this. Or maybe you'd prefer a quiet evening here, just as you want."

She did not have the will or strength to resist.

*****

As Paul showed her the city over the next few days, she became aware of a growing consciousness of him: the carefully shaven fragrant cheek as he sat close to her in the car; the vividness of the dark hairline against his caramel skin in the flickering street lights' glow; his easy manner with the restaurant staff as they conducted them to the best seats; his voice – clear, low, engulfing her with a warmth that had nothing to do with the sun. She was halfway to falling in love with him, more than halfway. If she tried to dig her heels in now, she'd lose her balance. As she fell asleep (with some difficulty) thoughts of him raced around her mind and he was her first blistering thought when she awoke. *"It's just the situation,"* she concluded. *"I'm a stranger in a strange land, and he is my refuge. It's merely my instinct for self-preservation kicking in."* But she struggled to explain away the attention to detail he devoted to her wellbeing; physical, occupational and, yes, emotional. When they left to fly to Mumbai, she was dismayed to find herself believing that this sweetness would disappear when they left India to return home.

She also felt an unexpected sadness to leave Kunal, Priya (who had acted as her personal maid – what luxury!), the two guys who waited at table and the rest of the obliging staff. Yet they displayed no abjection, just simple dignity as they concerned themselves with their duties. Quite often she had mistaken them for family members. She learnt that Paul had two younger stepsisters, three aunts and some others of an indeterminate relationship that she was never able to understand. But everyone in the household was unfailingly polite and constantly smiling. They seemed pleased to have her company. She never detected any long-harboured resentment at the colonial past. But then, as she learnt, the local nobility had generally done rather well out of the arrangement, with little loss of power and some enhanced international prestige.

*****

For their last evening in Bangalore, they enjoyed a meal in an eye-wateringly expensive restaurant. As well as its beautifully appointed dining area, it had an adjoining room full of soft, plump sofas for lounging back and smoking the traditional shishas or Hubble bubble pipes.

"Is this an opium den?" Kimberley asked in hushed tones as she was clearing her dessert plate, and couldn't identify the tantalising odours drifting across.

"Not this one. They're just smoking tobacco, usually flavoured. Want to try?"

They moved across with their coffee, and the waiters brought the hookah and lit the charcoal in the metal tray below the tobacco container. She took a deep draught as she simultaneously took a sly satisfaction in being the only woman participating. Gorgeous! The warm moist tobacco smoke smelt and tasted of apple and cinnamon. Kimberley lay back on the cushions with astonished pleasure.

"I hate smoking usually, but this could convert me. Do you do this regularly?"

He laughed. "Once in a while. I have everything at home, and sometimes I join visitors in a smoke. So you like it?"

"I love it! But this is a one-off. I suspect I could easily get addicted."

"I can't believe you would. But now that you're in a mellow mood, I have a present for you back in the car. I hope it fits."

Another surprise! But this one was very different; a package containing Indian women's clothing. Not a sari but a heavily embroidered and bejewelled tunic, tight satin trousers and a shimmering chiffon wrap to wear as a trailing scarf. All in shades of grey, gold and blue. Kimberley threw her arms around Paul's neck with exclamations of delight. She'd admired the passing girls in their richly coloured outfits – eye-catching, discreet but at the same time, oh! so alluring.

"How can I ever thank you?"

"Just give me your firstborn son, that'll be enough," he replied drolly.

Later that night, she tried on everything in her room and loved the new image. It was only, as she was falling asleep that she started wondering at the reason for the gift. Did Paul find her clothing style disappointing? Or even offensive? Was it simply a case of trying to please her with a predictably satisfying present for a woman? Or was there a message? Would he prefer her to be of his race and culture?

*****

In Mumbai they were more like conventional tourists, hiring taxis for travel and staying in the Four Seasons Hotel – but still in separate rooms, mind. Just as well, because her solitary hours were still occupied from time to time with memories of that wonderful night with James. Instead of fuelling fond memories, it now pricked her conscience, like a fish bone caught in her throat. Paul's steadfast resistance to any kind of romantic advance she found puzzling. The power he held over her family's future dissuaded her from taking any initiative so that she could never be accused of gold-digging or other sinister manipulation – above all by herself. But not even a goodnight kiss?

Paul's wealth and rank obviously carried much less weight here with the car firm's management. The original appointment, arranged before they travelled, was cancelled and there was endless confusion about fixing another. It amused Kimberley to see how irritated Paul became at the delays. He fretted that the deal could become irretrievable, although it was strange that he should be so determined to achieve something that seemed to hold little gain for himself.

The extra time allowed them to explore the tourist areas of Mumbai. At Paul's urging, they would ride in the quaint, noisy auto rickshaws, careering down narrow backstreets, where the combined fragrance of roasting spices made their heads spin and stomachs pulse with anticipation. The evenings were much more tranquil with quiet dinners either in the hotel or upmarket restaurants.

"The new police chief here is a bit overzealous," explained Paul. "He promotes sudden and unannounced raids on nightclubs and bars, then arrests and strip searches the customers. Up to one thousand in one event. They are usually accused of drugs, prostitution and other criminal offences and some held in custody for weeks. It's reckoned that the police are just jealous, but there is undoubtedly real concern about the lack of morality in the young and rich."

"So you would be of no interest to them, of course."

Kimberley remembered to persuade him to take her to an Indian temple. They accessed it through a series of broad but busy alleys. Indian people may not be the fastest movers in the world but they always seemed to be purposefully up to something. Rather like cats. As they neared the temple, stalls lined the sides selling nick-nacks, snacks and vehemently coloured flowers – masses and masses of them, in glorious colours, woven into blazing garlands draped across the sides, fronts and canopies of the merchants' stalls. While they were hopeful of selling to passers-by, they did not seem overly pushy.

"Do you want to buy any?"

Kimberley started. Why ever would she? Was she expected, to actively participate in the worship? And what did it all signify? Would it be simply a polite sharing of the indigenous custom or a hypocritical renunciation of her own cultural beliefs?

"Er, no thanks," she mumbled with some embarrassment. But at least Paul did not buy any either.

The temple now came into view, not very large or impressive from the outside. A straggle of beggars loitered in the area immediately before it and approached them warily for alms. She saw Paul surreptitiously slip something into the hand of one.

"Does the temple help them?"

"No, they rely solely on the generosity of the worshippers."

"And what did you give that one? Money?"

Paul looked sheepish. "Yes, he was blind, so he needed the help." No further discussion.

They progressed into the temple and, removing their shoes, joined a queue to view the shrine, shuffling round to view the god. Within a large carved gothic enclosure was a sculptured figure of the elephant-headed Ganesh surrounded by a host of garish representations of an earthly pastoral scene – animals, trees, fantastic flowers and shrubs. The priests received the gifts from the crowd, draping garlands around the god and over some of the items. All the ethereal beauty lay in these transient flowers, not in soaring stone for eternity. The profusion of plants was gorgeous but seemed gross, somehow – too redolent of earthly delights for the great monotheistic religions. And what happened when every place was full? The areas selected by the priests were already looking overloaded. Were they then passed back to the traders outside and recycled? Or trashed?

When folks had made their offerings most retreated and sat in the rows of wooden benches arranged in a semicircle before the shrine while yet more crowds filled their place, thrusting their gifts at the busy priests.

Kimberley looked around her. Temple helpers stood by with besoms to keep the place swept. At the sides of the area stood yet more sales pitches but these were marketing trinkets, incense and a variety of statuettes of Ganesh and other animal gods, all painted in bright colours, nothing subtle in sight. Across from the entrance area stood some kind of large, pewter-coloured lump surrounded by people. After a while, she worked out, that it was a huge metal rat and people were taking turns to bend over and whisper in its ears. Paul saw the direction of her gaze as he ushered her to a space which became vacant in the seating.

"That's a silver rat, and he's the servant of Ganesh. Whatever your heart desires, you whisper in its ear and he will pass the message on to the god and help you get it."

"Maybe someone should desire to clean it," she thought.

"What would you whisper?" he asked.

Kimberley thought for a moment. "That you would be successful with this car firm and the deal goes ahead. The family needs it."

Yes, it would stop Irene prostituting herself with lascivious rich gigolos like George Quirke. Kimberley had fully understood the reasons for the affair. Irene was calculating. Never mind her protests about being lonely since David's death. At her age, that couldn't matter, could it? And, anyway, Irene could command, sorry, attract any man she wanted; she had looks, style and, most of all, money.

"And I want Bob to be okay, to sort himself out." Her thought harked back to the last fraught telephone call.

There was a long pause as they continued to watch the shuffling crowd.

"Nothing else?" asked Paul

Kimberley looked at him. Was there uncertainty in his eyes? A pleading? Vulnerability? Amid the murmuring bustle and faintly pleasant smell of incense and warm bodies, she felt suddenly anxious. Fearful, almost. That penetrating gaze of his required a response. But what?

"What is it that *you* want, Paul? What would you whisper?"

There was a long pause, then he spoke very quietly. She could hardly hear him and doubted the words.

"My desire is that you would marry me."

Chapter 10

As Kimberley sat in the plane her mind was still in turmoil. She idly twirled a strand of hair with her fingers; it was now bleached by the sun to that attractive corn colour that can never be produced by artifice. Multiple thoughts swarmed around seeking attention, like a litter of hungry piglets searching for a sow's teats. The simile entertained her.

The largest and most demanding piglet was Paul's marriage proposal. His voice had been soft and sweet yet confident. The hustle and devout intensity in the temple around them had dropped away leaving the scene imprinted on her memory in stark clarity. She had swallowed down the end of her exclamation that began: "But we haven't even –", feeling that a temple, even one in pragmatic, fecund India, was hardly the place to plead the questionable advantages of exploratory fornication.

"– We hardly know each other," she finished lamely.

"But we're working on that all the time," he countered.

The prospect of marrying this gorgeous rich demi-god might be the stuff of idle daydreams but the reality was much more complex, her motives included. That merited some assessment. To what extent was her attraction for him swayed by externalities? Like unimaginable wealth?

Another forceful piglet was James. Barely a week had passed since they... Kimberley's thoughts veered towards fantasy as the memory bloomed again until guilt prompted her to glance at Paul by her side. She studied him as he leafed through the in-flight magazine. A night's glorious passion – with more to come? – versus an unknown life in India, albeit one of luxury. Possibly stifling luxury. Was this a trade she cared to make right now? She just didn't know.

Piglets less successful at grabbing time on the teat were Bob (no news from him or Richard since she'd been away), Lisa (no hoped-for gesture of reconciliation or word if she's been accepted on her nursing course yet) and Irene. The atmosphere at home had been icy with barely a word spoken between them before she'd left. It was left to Richard, dull, level-headed, non-judgmental Richard to act as mediator.

Squeezed out as the runt with hardly any suckling at all were the family business troubles. This was rather surprising, as Paul had assured her that the Indian firm was amenable to reconsidering the deal. The family's future would be secure, and it would remove any excuse for George Quirke to stick his nose or his money (not to mention his cock) into the family affairs. Surely Irene would kick him out then?

Back in for another feed came the marriage proposal piglet. She'd asked for time to think it over, giving all sorts of spontaneous, plausible reasons for her hesitation. It amused her to see how an unsuspected streak of vanity in him had difficulty with her prevarication. It was rather like finding damage to the frame of the Mona Lisa. But he had insisted on a deadline for her decision of one month; a reasonable period, she conceded.

It was Monday morning when she arrived home, so Irene and Richard were at work when the taxi dropped her at Prospect Hall. She returned the exuberant welcome from the dogs, collected some mail from the hall table and slowly climbed the stairs to unpack. Before she had time to come back down to the kitchen to get herself a coffee the landline telephone rang. It was George Quirke.

"And did my favourite Weatherby enjoy her holiday in India?"

'Favourite' Weatherby? If he was sleeping with Irene, where did this leave her? Her professional manner kicked in and, with a smile in her voice, she tried to answer as civilly as she could. No sense in alienating a potential rescuer – or step-parent. Good, God! There was no chance that this was serious with Irene, was there? Like, *marriage*? She did not doubt that Irene would be quite prepared to go down that route to secure her business ambitions.

George had travelled to India a few years ago to review some investments first hand and was eager to exchange reminiscences so there was no way she could quickly terminate the conversation. He'd stayed in Mumbai and seen all the things that would-be cultured people should see, but the opinions were patently second-hand, as though the viewing was through others' eyes and not his own. She listened patiently until she could remind him that Irene was at work, but it seemed that it was Kimberley whom he wanted to speak with, anyway. Lisa had been accepted onto a nursing course in London and had won a grant from a health charity – with George's help, of course. Also, he had been influential in her being accepted for part-time work in reception at a central London hospital. Combined with a student loan, she was going to be able to fund her studies admirably as long as she didn't mind hard work. Kimberley believed that the arrangements would suit Lisa very well and she found herself feeling warm gratitude towards the repulsive slime ball as she thanked him. What he expected in return she didn't dare imagine. But he was looking forward to seeing her tomorrow evening when he would be calling round. What a pity that she was going to have to work late to catch up on the week she was away…but, never mind, he would be seeing her anyway when he called round next weekend. Kimberley could almost hear him slobbering with anticipation. She acquiesced as graciously as she could before ringing off with relief. Still, it was good news about Lisa.

James must still be travelling abroad. She was finishing leaving a voicemail for him when she heard a car pull up at the front entrance. She wandered along to the hallway and, to her astonishment, saw Richard helping Irene from her car. From the way Richard was assisting, with his arm about her shoulders, it was clear that her stepmother was in a shocked state.

"What's happened?"

Irene did not answer, visibly distraught and shaking.

"Bob's been killed," said Richard. "Fire at a nightclub in the early hours of Sunday morning. Bad state. Get the kettle on."

The next few hours were the toughest Kimberley could remember. A black, nauseous cloud enshrouded her. Dead! Bob – so carefree, teasing, vital. She stood paralysed with horror at how it could have happened.

"Cup of tea, Kim," urged Richard gently, his usual stoicism prey to the novelty of showing concern for others' distress. While she fumbled with the kettle – barely seeing what she was doing through a veil of suppressed tears – Irene sat down at the big table as if mesmerised, clutching first her handbag and then the mug of tea as though it were the key to life itself. Richard's face was a livid mask as he hovered around them fidgeting with the car keys which, for some obscure logic, he refused to relinquish. The conversation was minimal, strangled and monosyllabic.

Why? *Why*? There was no sense in it. Only the good die young, they say. So he *was* good, worthy, valued. Fate had validated this. But the idea was a weak consolation. His death was devastating. Absolutely devastating.

She looked across at Irene while clumsily wiping some spilt water from the worktop. It must be even worse for her – her only child, dying before her. Monstrous injustice. Unwonted sympathy for her stepmother fought with her own grief.

No one seemed to know how it had happened, reported Richard. The police had said that most of the victims were taken to the hospital in ambulances but apart from smoke inhalation, few were in a critical condition. It wasn't even certain yet that one of the fatalities was Bob. Identification arose from items found on him – phone, wallet, bank cards. Richard was going to have to formally identify the body.

When this was mentioned, Irene looked across at him with a mixture of grief, wonder and, yes, hatred.

"There shall no evil befall thee, neither shall any plague come nigh thy dwelling. For he shall give his angels charge over thee, to keep thee in all thy ways. They shall bear thee up in their hands, lest thou dash thy foot against a stone."

The two children stared at Irene as she quoted the Psalm in a dull monotone. But she wasn't doing it to win their attention. She dropped her gaze to stare down at the table and continued in the same tone, but more softly.

"God lies! He breaks his promises. I'll never, never trust him again." Then she raised her head and glared at Richard. "Why couldn't it have been you!" She was almost shouting. "My only child! And all I've got left are some other woman's spawn!" She spat the words out at them, then collapsed into body-racking sobs while Kimberley's and Richard's eyes met in stunned silence.

*****

Two days later Richard flew to London to identify the body. In a subdued telephone conversation with Kimberley afterwards he did not elaborate on the difficulty. The face and hands were badly burnt. There was no trace left even of Bob's luxuriant hair. But the features were recognisable enough for the most fleeting glance to know they belonged to Bob.

Over the next few days problems were emerging before Richard began the harrowing task of arranging the repatriation and funeral. At the post-mortem, traces of alcohol were found in the body – no surprise there – but also a large amount of cocaine. The police were unwilling to release any of the bodies – there were five sad victims – before the inquest into the fire which would be held shortly. The family had to be content to wait while they absorbed their grief.

The house had a deathly hush on it. Despite a multitude of callers who paid their respects either in person or by telephone, the very walls seemed to have ingested a deep, pervasive sorrow. Both Kimberley and Irene spent most of their time apart in their rooms. Kimberley spent hours gazing out of her window at the deteriorating autumn weather. It was so wrong, so unnatural; the sun shone and the rain rained on all humanity, but nothing could pretend to be the same as before. Everyone else could carry on as usual. The rest of the world was unaffected. Callous.

She had called in at her work the next day, but before she had even told of the tragedy, she was ushered into the branch manager's office and quietly advised that her services were no longer needed. Unapproved holidays taken at irresponsibly short notice combined with the business's need to downsize due to a lack of sales were the reasons given. When she at last delivered her own news, she rather enjoyed their guilty embarrassment. It was some compensation for the twinge of regret she felt at the rejection. But only momentarily. There was too much going on in her life at the moment to care about something so trivial as earning a living. They cordially agreed on the terms of separation. Compassionate leave combined with gardening leave meant she no longer needed to come to the office. They could telephone her to iron out any ongoing matters or she could call in as needed. She could complete the deal for Paul's house.

Not that she'd spoken to him since their return. He had rung several times but as soon as his caller ID had shown, she had switched the call to voicemail. Although she felt both guilt and ingratitude doing it, the relationship was emotionally loaded enough. It might not bear any more heartache.

By the time Saturday morning came, some of the shock of the tragedy had subsided and the burden of apathy began to replace piercing grief. Kimberley had begun to miss the routine of work. The waiting seemed aimless. As she wandered down to the kitchen to make a cup of coffee – the persistent nausea had relented now – and consider whether she wanted to commit any effort to prepare some lunch, the doorbell rang. She glimpsed a taxi drawn up outside as she opened the door.

"Paul!" She did not want this meeting. "What are you doing here?"

His demeanour was quite different from the usual. Unsure. Diffident.

"I only read the local newspaper this morning." He held it out tentatively. The front-page headline screamed: *'Local family business heir killed in nightclub horror.'*

Kimberley raised her hands to obscure the tears that immediately welled up. At the same time, Paul stepped forward and wrapped his arms around her. She succumbed to the enveloping warmth and cried. Real tears now, the first since it had happened. She sobbed into his chest as her body weakened in his embrace.

It cannot have been long before Irene's stentorian voice sounded. "Who is it?"

Neither replied and after a while her steps were heard, approaching along the hallway.

"What are you doing here?"

"It's okay," began Kimberley as she choked back the tears, but Paul interrupted.

"I came as soon as I heard about Bob."

"So, now you know, you can leave. Right now."

Paul's eyebrows lifted a fraction at the unfriendly welcome but he didn't move.

"I also wanted to talk with you about business."

"We have nothing to talk about. Please go now."

"Please listen before you dismiss me. What I have to say could be of value to you."

Irene pursed her lips and glared at him. "All right. What is it?"

"Can we talk in private?"

"Why? There are no business secrets from Kimberley. She is a director of the company."

Kimberley sensed that her presence might limit the interchange even more than it promised. She made to excuse herself and pulled away from Paul.

But Irene's curiosity was piqued and she indicated that Paul should follow her to the study. Kimberley loitered between the hall and kitchen, wondering whether cups of coffee would be advisable. It seemed unlikely but she could have one herself, anyway. And she could splash her eyes with cold water to reduce their red swelling.

No chance! Any conversation must have finished very shortly after it began. The door opened suddenly and Paul emerged rapidly. Irene was quivering with anger as she ushered him to the door.

Kimberley was puzzled. Surely the decision by the Indians to reopen negotiations would be top of the list. Other matters such as the disputed parcel of land or his identity could not have been covered in the time taken.

"When your house is more welcoming than your manners, it is a sad state of affairs."

"Many an ass has entered Jerusalem," scowled Irene as she shot venomous eyes at Kimberley. "If you marry him, it's at your peril!" she hissed, shrilly.

So that's the reason for her anger!. Why on earth did Paul mention it? What has he been saying?

"I haven't decided myself, yet." Kimberley wanted to reclaim some control of the situation.

Paul stopped before crossing the doorstep. "Kimberley has every right to choose whom she will marry," then, turning to the daughter: "Your welcome just now told me your answer," he said softly.

"Think carefully, Kimberley! You have no job now – don't lose your home as well!" Acid. "And I can disinherit you, remember!"

"Are you coming to lunch?" queried Paul, unfazed by the threats issuing from his would-be stepmother-in-law.

Kimberley hesitated momentarily, wondering whether to go and throw in her lot with a possibly pressurising escort or endure staying at home with a venomous Irene. Rock and a hard place. This choice could have formidable repercussions.

"I'll just get my things," and she went upstairs for her coat and handbag.

*****

Neither spoke during the taxi journey. Each mulled over the implications of Irene's dazzling display of fury. Kimberley expected that Paul would press her on the marriage decision. Instead, his conversation was casual and unthreatening, successfully eschewing both the banal and the pressured. When he didn't, she dared to broach the subject as they lunched at the Tanroagan.

"Why on earth did you mention the marriage proposal? You must know that it was toxic."

Paul grinned and sly mischief suffused his face. "Perverseness." Then he giggled. Yes, actually *giggled*. This was a new side of the man that Kimberley had not seen before.

"I began by explaining that the Indian firm was agreeable to re-negotiating the deal but she didn't want to know. No matter what I said, she wouldn't listen. She kept saying it was impossible without the extra land. I tried to tell her that there may be a way round that. I even considered disclosing who I am but she was determined not to listen to anything I said. Then, quite unexpectedly, she announced that the business was going to get a massive injection of capital that would secure its future. Did you know about this?"

"O my God! This must be from Gruesome George," she thought. Then aloud, "No. Irene doesn't discuss her plans with the family. She's not what you would call a team player."

"I see. Well, after announcing this, she sat there so smug and arrogant, that I just wanted to squash that complacency. So I said that we were getting married. But I didn't expect she would react as she did. She immediately got up, swearing loudly – I thought she was going to physically attack me. If I hadn't got out of there as quickly as I did, I think she would have thrown me out!"

Kimberley laughed. The first time this week. She found the account hugely amusing. It was impossible for mortal man to put one over on her stepmother.

Paul's merriment faded. "What did Irene mean when she said you had no job?"

"Oh, I quit. They didn't like me going away at short notice and business is very slow. I think they were glad to have an excuse to get rid of someone."

"So your trip lost you your job?"

Kimberley shrugged. "Not really. And your house purchase won't be affected, don't worry."

"She also said about disinheriting you. Can she do that?"

"I doubt it. She's upset and confused at the moment. She'll probably disinherit the dogs and take me to the vet's to be put to sleep. Especially if I marry you. I have a trust fund set up under my father's will but I can't touch that till I'm thirty. Richard's the same. I suspect he's relying on that to pay for a new marital home next year. I can't imagine Julie wanting to live at Prospect Hall."

"But what about now? Do you have any income?" Kimberley did not care for Paul to learn about her private financial affairs. Not yet. But her mind started considering her position. For now, at least, she did have a roof over her head and some final salary and commission still due from work. When would that come?

"I understand you've exchanged contracts on the house. Do you know when you will complete the purchase?"

"Next week. Then I shall have to buy some things for it. If you have the time, I'm hoping you'll help me."

Kimberley nodded slowly. "The vendor's moved his things out already. Do you want to see it again? It will help you decide what you want."

She arranged to collect the keys and take him for a second viewing straightaway. Stripped of its furnishings, the house echoed around them. The rooms seemed bigger but colder. Maybe the weather was less kind than when they first looked round. They ended up in the kitchen, shadowy in the fading afternoon light.

"Do you want to replace the white goods?" she asked, flicking open the door of a smelly old fridge as Paul gazed out of the window at the tiny private garden. Her voice held a trace of coquetry.

"What do you suggest?" He smiled, came across and slipped an arm around her waist. Then he kissed her gently. It was breathtakingly pleasant. He continued to kiss her several times, dispelling her gloom as thoroughly as the sun had dissipated the mist earlier that morning.

"Have I told you that I love you?" he murmured. His voice was the merest whisper as he bent his face nearer to hers.

"Er – not that I can remember. You could do it now."

"I'd rather show you."

His arms pulled her close to him until she could feel the warmth of his skin through his shirt front. Then his mouth pressed hard against hers and his arms held her even closer so she could hardly breathe. She wove her hands around his neck, feeling the taut muscles underneath and pressed her body into his. Then she pulled back slightly, feeling the urgency of his intention. Her heart was racing like some frightened animal.

"Not so fast," she thought to herself, *"I'm no pushover."* Independence and defiance battled with arousal. His eyes were almost closed as he edged her along until she was leaning against the tall larder fridge.

"We belong to each other," he stated quietly but with disturbing confidence. She felt herself give, soften. His hands slid down her back, gently pulled off her jacket. All the sadness and frustration of recent weeks evaporated in that instant. Even James' image faded away. The room receded, the whole cosmos dwindled from her consciousness. Her own hands responded, searching for his body. And there, right there against an old Smeg, he made love to her. Powerfully.

140

Insistently. Rhythmically. Not so much animal spirits as a sweet fulfilment. She clung to him in a fiery storm of sensation. Passion drenched her senses in the hot wine of pleasure.

Kimberley wasn't even aware of the cold hard handle digging into her back until some time afterwards.

Chapter 11

If you asked people what image the words 'rich' and 'blubber' conjured up, they might say Bill Gates' children bewailing their curtailed inheritance. For Kimberley, it was the sight of George Quirke in just trousers and vest (a *vest* – did men still wear them?) leaning against the kitchen doorway.

She had returned home late and stealthily to a quiet house last night. Rising early (for a Sunday), she wandered down to the kitchen in her dressing gown. The mornings were becoming chilly. She was fixing her morning cup of coffee, waiting for the kettle to boil and humming blissfully until she saw him.

His head was tipped to one side. "And why is the lovely young Miss Weatherby so happy in these troubled days?"

Damn! What convincing reason could she give? "I'm just glad that Irene has someone to comfort her."

He looked sceptical.

"– and that the business will have the capital it needs to give it a secure future." *That* brought a sly, smug smile to his face!

"It's not Irene who's my chief concern," he drawled with a meaningful look straight at her. This did not look promising.

A change of mood was needed. "Would you like a cup of coffee or tea?" she inquired brightly.

"That's very kind of you, Kimberley," he said as he moved over to where she stood, close enough to slide an arm around her shoulders and then abruptly thrust his slobbery lips down on hers. He smelt like a used cat litter tray. She had enough presence of mind to jerk her head away as soon as she realised what was happening, so he missed his target a bit; her cheek was getting a good chewing. So gross! Then he grabbed her head with his other fleshy paw and forced it around until his lips reached their goal. He was strong, she couldn't wriggle away. Moreover, despite her distaste for the rubbery, nicotine-flavoured sensation, she was reluctant to struggle too strenuously. After all, apart from helping her former best friend, this was the saviour of the family business and – heaven forbid! – possibly her future stepfather. Then she felt his hand moving down and fumbling at the neck opening of her dressing gown. Dear God! What was coming next?

And that was how Irene caught them. Kimberley quickly extricated herself with a combination of dexterity and tact.

"Get out!" Irene snarled, her eyes flashing scalding wrath, "Both of you!"

George let go only slowly. "Irene, love –" he began.

"Out of my house!" she shouted. "And that includes you, Kimberley!"

Kimberley needed no further urging. She scurried upstairs to her room, rubbing her hand repeatedly over her lips to remove the taint and slobber.

The realisation that she was being made technically homeless was a novel and unpleasant thought as she sat on the edge of her bed, shaking intermittently at the shock of the whole situation. Was that really what Irene intended? Did wicked stepmothers throw out their acquired-by-marriage daughters these days? Or banish them to menial duties, à la Cinderella? That was ridiculous. She couldn't mean it. But what if she did? What could Kimberley do and where would she go? Maybe when she helped Paul choose items for his house, she would be choosing them for herself. No! Rushing headlong into co-habitation simply because of problems at home seemed a stupid way to conduct one's life. Maybe Julie's flat was a safer option for now. But first, let's see if Irene means it. She lay down on the bed – still a bit warm! – plagued by random thoughts on the topic, interrupted by memories of last night. How could life deliver such opposing experiences in such quick succession? Nothing could be heard from the kitchen so Kimberley could only guess what was happening. It was nearly an hour before Irene opened the bedroom door. Kimberley swung her legs over the side of the bed and got up to face her.

"Shouldn't you knock? Or did you think I'd left home already?"

Irene started, then entered unbidden, sighed and sat down on the bed. Kimberley had never seen her look so drained. It was like looking at a bleak, frozen mask with no actual person behind it.

"We need to talk, Kimberley," she said slowly, as though she had difficulty with the whole idea, not just getting the words out.

Despite her anxiety, Kimberley was disturbed to see her stepmother so distressed. She considered what response would be appropriate. "How about over a cup of coffee? My earlier one was interrupted. Though goodness knows what story George has fed you."

When they were seated at the kitchen table with their drinks in front of them, the tension lessened.

"I didn't encourage him. I swear to you. It was a complete surprise. Shock, rather." Kimberley shuddered at the memory. "How could you let him even touch you!"

She saw Irene's cheek muscles clench and her hands trembled as she looked at them spread around the hot cup. This was not the best approach.

"You didn't seem to be struggling much yourself. But, no, it was probably mainly him." The words seemed to choke her. There was a cold hostility.

"Mainly him! Why, he –" but she broke off as Irene screwed up her eyes in exasperation. It was foolish to think that she hadn't already sussed out the man.

"Declaiming from the moral high ground is rarely attractive or convincing, Kimberley. You're very young and, frankly, with no great experience of men, I think, so I must make allowances for that. You probably cannot recognise mere flirtation for what it is."

"Flirtation! He was about to –"

Irene gave her a bitter look. Kimberley bridled at her stepmother's refusal to recognise a potential rape situation, then realised it was almost certainly meant to include a latent criticism of her relationship with Paul as well. But she kept quiet. Arguing the point would achieve nothing right now.

Irene continued but the voice had a softer tone. "Quite apart from any personal relationship, George can inject a considerable sum of money into the business. We are just one step away from bankruptcy. With his help, even without the land and distributorship, we could continue for probably another two years. Believe me, things are getting pretty desperate. As it is, I am going to have to announce some redundancies tomorrow."

The bitch! That would mean Lisa's mother, who worked as a cleaner could be targeted. That family wasn't having any luck. "I don't understand. If we just tighten our belts, surely we can tick over until the economy picks up again. After all, the family could supply any additional working capital to keep us going."

Irene raised her chin a fraction and pursed her lips. "I've obviously done a good job in presenting the accounts over the last couple of years. The truth is, Kimberley, that the family doesn't have any more money. I've been subsidising the company from my personal funds since not long after your father died. That money is now gone. Why do you think I've not replaced Anna? The pregnancy was a very convenient excuse. Do you think I like cooking? And cleaning? What's more, the house is now mortgaged up to the hilt. Bob's insatiable requests for money did not help."

"So you don't know about his debts."

"What debts?"

"It's about time someone told you that Bob was under suspicion of embezzlement of the Student Union funds. I don't know how much was involved but I do know that he did seem to follow an extravagant lifestyle at uni."

"My God! Is there no end to it!" Irene whispered as she covered her ashen face with her hands. Neither spoke for several minutes, each unwilling to increase the fraught contemplation of a wrecked life, "Bob had the ability to disregard all the unpleasant consequences of his actions and a total inability to foresee them."

Then Irene raised her head with defiance in her eyes. "At the moment, I'm struggling to service all the debts. But George's money would enable us to continue. It would mean that that pressure is lifted. We could stay in this house, for the moment, at least."

Kimberley got up to lean against the window sill (ignoring the tender spot in her back from yesterday's amatory activities) while she mulled over the consequences of the revelations.

Irene continued in a very low voice. "However, there are strings attached. I have to admit that I misread the situation. Now I know I was wrong. You see, George's money is conditional on you marrying him."

Kimberley gasped and stared at her stepmother. Now her face was also an ashen hue. For a long moment neither spoke.

"You're joking! Aren't you? He's the last person on earth I'd marry! My worst nightmare! He's repulsive!"

Irene sat silent and immobile.

"I cannot believe I'm hearing this – it's like a something out of a trashy novel a hundred years ago. People just don't do this anymore. No, of course, I won't marry him." Then, as an afterthought, "He probably just wants to get hold of my money anyway." She walked over to the door and opened it to leave.

"You'd get hold of all his."

Kimberley stopped and looked at Irene sharply. "Oh, yes, I'm sure the pre-nuptial agreement would allow that! Don't be so stupid – it's not me that's naïve, but you! Or –" Kimberley let go of the door and leant over Irene. "Is this whole idea cooked up by you to get *your* hands on his money? To sacrifice the family and save both the business *and* your precious reputation?"

Irene turned away in disgust. "Of course not!"

"Why do I not believe you?" Kimberley moved back towards the door and stood facing Irene.

"So your answer's 'No' then?"

"Correct!"

"Well, then, in that case, I'll go ahead and announce the redundancy programme tomorrow and put the house on the market. Though I cannot see anyone buying it with the market in its present depressed state. If we don't get a serious offer within two months, the bank will repossess it and it will probably be auctioned. Then we'll all be homeless. Happy with that?"

"If the alternative is marrying George Quirke, yes I am. You bet I am!"

Irene rose.

"What I don't understand is why you wouldn't listen to Paul. He's got a solution to the extra land problem that would allow the Indian distributorship to go ahead. He's arranged that as well. And I suspect he could help with any interim working capital, too. Please give him a hearing. Then George wouldn't be needed – not for his money, anyway."

Irene remained unmoved. She lowered her head. "It's not just the money. You cannot understand my situation. I loved your father and we were very happy together. Since the accident, my life has been very lonely. As though my heart was a stone. The pain was deep, an ongoing ache that persisted all the time so that I forgot what life was like without it. I wouldn't wish it on anyone, and I hope you will never have to go through anything similar. I thought you could replace a husband easier than a son. Now I'm not so sure."

Kimberley's eyes widened. Was this confession time? Irene never went in for heart-to-hearts with anybody. This conversation was revealing hidden depths.

Irene continued with a tender intonation that Kimberley had never heard or even imagined. "You're not the only one who's lain awake at night wishing your man was lying beside you, longing for his touch." Her voice had become barely audible. "In an ideal world, no, George would not be my choice either, but his attention is – was – flattering, I admit it. I misunderstood the whole thing. I thought it meant more to him than it did. That *I* meant more to him. But it seems he was using me to get to you. And, yes, I admit that his promise to inject capital into the business was a factor. It meant we could at least keep a roof over our heads. Anyone would have done the same as me."

"Like hell, they would," thought Kimberley, but she knew that arguing the case at this stage would achieve nothing. "So do you still want me to leave?"

"No. Of course I don't – but if you do stay," Irene raised her head and shot her stepdaughter a defiant look, "make sure you don't bring that man to the house again."

Kimberley suppressed a protest. She did not want to cave in and agree to that, even with the unspoken threat of being turfed out of her home if he did turn up. Just as well Irene did not try to forbid any marriage to him, which was looking increasingly like a good idea. "I suspect your threat of disinheriting me is a bit thin from what you've told me. So be it. Apart from that, I was hoping that I could work in the business, too. Maybe in marketing – sales are a problem area, and I'm pretty good at that. Even if I do say so myself. No one else in this family will."

Irene dropped her gaze and shook her head a little. "We'll discuss that another time. The last thing I want is to take on another employee. I have a lot to think over right now." She turned to place the mugs in the sink.

"I expect you want to get ready for church now." Doubtfully.

"No. Never again. It doesn't work, does it? There isn't any God, after all. And even if there is, he doesn't do anything. He – or she – is no use to anyone."

Irene walked out of the room with something akin to her usual dignity.

*****

The family's breakfast on Monday morning was a dull affair until Richard walked in and announced, "Guess what! Late last night, I received a text from Frederick Galbraith. I didn't even know he knew my mobile number."

"I didn't know he knew how to text," observed Kimberley.

"Why would he get in touch? What did it say?" said Irene.

"Let me read it to you: Ballaclucas land now available for sale or rent. Will advise terms shortly via solicitors."

They all exchanged looks of astonishment.

"Do we want it now, though?" asked Richard. "Without the Indian deal, it's just a useless and probably hugely expensive investment."

"I think I have the solution to that problem," piped up Kimberley. "When I was in India, my – er – a friend had a meeting with them and I know they were agreeable to resume negotiations."

Irene looked unconvinced. "Even if we could go ahead, it wouldn't be immediately. We'd need to find the funds not just for the purchase or lease, but also the working capital to tide us over till then." She looked pointedly across the table to Kimberley. "Business is still poor. I wonder what's caused this sudden change of heart."

"Maybe they need the money," suggested Richard.

"Seems a bit unlikely. Before we do anything else, I think we'd better speak to Lady Galbraith."

"Do you want me to do that?" volunteered Richard. "I don't wish to be provocative, but she's more likely to talk to me. After all, you two haven't spoken in years."

"Yes, that might be a good idea. Let me have a little time to think it over. We'll discuss what you can say at the office. I can listen in or even speak to her if needed."

"As long as you don't put her in a bad mood."

"She's been in a bad mood for twenty years. For her to get in a good mood, she'd have to drown some puppies or something."

Chapter 12

"We thought it would be better to delay the wedding till next year. That way, anyone wearing morning dress would be reflecting a time of day rather than a state of bereavement." Julie looked pleased with her pun. "Probably Easter."

"Or in the school summer holidays," said Richard. Having made the monumental decision to marry, he seemed in no great hurry to execute the deed. "And we're not inviting any guests. Half of them only come for the beer and the other half just want to get drunk."

Kimberley was astonished at this new-found levity in her formerly solemn brother. "Do you know yet where you're going to live?" she asked.

"Not at Prospect Hall!" declared Julie with a toss of her head.

"Wouldn't your flat be suitable? I thought it was charming," suggested Paul.

They were taking a quick lunch in the town centre the following Friday. At an Indian restaurant, of course. Kimberley had decided that since she was remaining at Prospect Hall (at least for the moment) it was time for her to formally introduce Paul to the remaining members of the family with no distractions from accident-ridden pony rides or spurious gipsy fortune tellers.

"Oh no! I've taken it off the market for now but it's far too small anyway. It's not big enough for Tiffany and me, and now she's at school, she'll need her own space to invite her little school friends. And I would love to have room for a piano. I used to play, and Richard wants me to take it up again. So, as we've got the money, we thought the best way to invest it was in a large property with all the room we need."

"We haven't got the money yet," cautioned Richard reluctantly, pausing between mouthfuls.

"No, but we will have next April when you're thirty – plus the extra share of Bob's, of course."

Kimberley was astounded at this sudden mercenary manifestation from her friend. "How can you be sure of that?" she asked.

"Richard's checked the will. A dedicated sum was to be placed in trust and equally shared between the children. But now there are only two to share it – unfortunately." The last word was uttered rather too perfunctorily, Kimberley thought.

"But if Irene pops her clogs in the meantime…it's a moot point who will get the house." It was clear who was going to wear the trousers in this marriage – and probably the underpants as well. "If Irene's not there, well, living at Prospect Hall may not be so bad an idea. Don't you agree, Paul?" continued Julie invitingly. "Property is always a good investment."

Paul circumspectly broke off a piece of naan bread before he replied. "Not as good as a business, I would say. But investment here could be limited. Does the island have any strong growth sectors apart from software? What about other new technology?"

Unsuspecting, he'd hit upon Richard's love. "We do have a flourishing e-gaming sector and, surprisingly perhaps, a space industry. No, I'm serious. There are a lot of firms here, associated with satellite tracking, telemetry and optics as well as the relevant law and insurance. The industry's a major software customer, especially for telecoms. There's even a company here that's planning hotels that orbit the earth. Not budget hotels, I suspect and probably with no scheduled flights from Ronaldsway. The concept of special purpose vehicles to avoid tax takes on a whole new meaning. The government offers several worthwhile tax incentives. *Our* government, not the UK. The island was recently voted the fourth most likely country to launch an expedition to the moon. After the US, China and Russia. Two years ago we were only fifth."

"I thought the island was in the UK."

"Oh no! The British Isles, yes; our sovereign is the King, and we have common defence, for example. But in nearly all other matters, we're quite independent with a separate parliament. One that sets remarkably low income tax and corporation tax. And no CGT or stamp duty." Richard resumed his munching.

"And we have a monopoly on four-horned sheep and cats with no tails," added Julie in her best schoolmarm voice.

At that point Kimberley's mobile phone rang. She almost jumped when she saw that the caller was James, so she excused herself and went outside to answer it.

"Hi, James," she answered warmly. But there had been a momentary hesitation first. No longer did he haunt her fevered dreams.

"Hello, Kim. Yes, I'm back and I've got your messages. I've just come off the ferry and I'm driving home after a very successful trip. How about meeting up tonight when I can tell you about it? And we can catch up with some other things too." His tone made it quite clear what things stood at the top of his list. But despite some intense longing in the recent past, Kimberley felt no thrill of anticipation. Rather like the enticing aroma of coffee brewing that was followed by a disappointing bitterness on the tongue. And he obviously hadn't yet heard about Bob. Just how incommunicado had he been when overseas?

"Oh, what a shame! I've promised the girls I'd join them on a night out. Can I ring you tomorrow?" Even as she spun the lie, she knew she wouldn't ring him. Just as she knew she did not want to resurrect all the pain by telling him about Bob. They rang off with the usual affectionate pleasantries that, perversely, only made her eager to re-join the lunch party.

Richard was still expounding on the indisputable benefits of the island's independence when she returned. Julie was sitting back gazing vaguely at others in the restaurant and checking her watch from time to time. She would need to get back to school soon. To his credit, Paul was exhibiting some interest if somewhat bemused. Kimberley chose to change the subject to help him.

"Richard, have you talked to Lady Galbraith again about that land?"

"Now that's a house I wouldn't mind living in!" interjected Julie.

"Dream on," continued Richard. "Apart from Freddie, there could still be an heir or heiress in India. Sir Philip's daughter was also putting it about like the rest of the family. Still, good luck to them with that one."

Kimberley froze, avoiding Paul's gaze. But he continued with his meal unperturbed.

"Anyway, I talked with her just this morning, but there's no more news. And, despite leaving messages, she still hasn't heard from Freddie. She seems to be mellowing, though. This time she was almost chatty."

"All due to your seductive charm," crooned Julie, slipping her arm through his.

"Apparently he's repeatedly drawn huge sums of money from the company but is unavailable for any business decisions. He used his shareholding to make himself CEO after Sir Philip's death – with his mother's support, of course – but I bet now she wishes she hadn't. He just sends occasional texts. Whenever they ring him, his phone's always turned off."

"Doesn't he have a London address they could track him down at?"

"Yes, he has – or had – a posh flat in Chelsea. Lady G's just come back from trying that. The place is all shut up with a 'For Sale' notice outside. None of the neighbours has seen him recently at all. The solicitors are having the same problem. They have no new address for him so they send everything to the flat where he must be picking up his mail, probably at the dead of night. Then they get occasional texts back from him."

"Sounds a bit like Bob used to be. Sometimes I think they could almost be brothers. So, we can't move forward with the business at the moment," said Kimberley.

"I'm not sure it's the right move anyway. Back in the sixties, we used to make the world's smallest ever production car here on the Island: the P50. It was only a one-seater and handled like an inebriated chicken, I'm told. Only a few hundred were sold. There was talk of making it again but we've missed the boat. It's all about electric these days. Certainly we wouldn't be interested in distributing it. The Indian cars are similar in that they're aimed at a different market from ours."

Paul had listened with interest. "You mean the bottom end, don't you? The affordable end, you call it here. I think you're underestimating the potential of working with the Indians. I got the impression that it wasn't the current models they wanted you to distribute. I agree those are too unsophisticated for the British market. But things are changing. Like all Indian companies now, they are pouring a lot of money into innovation at a competitive price to win world markets. Hasn't the company discussed the new lines that are in the pipeline? They may suit the European market very well."

Richard admitted he knew nothing about this but doubted Irene did either. It looked as though blind growth had been her guiding motivation rather than a clever synergy of product and market. He began to mumble about extenuating factors but it was obvious that here was one member of the family who had not yet been convinced it was all a good idea.

Kimberley had been listening half-heartedly to the debate. Maybe now that she saw the family business as her future employer she should take a greater interest in company matters but she was still trying to make sense of her response to James' call. Why had she not been more delighted to hear from him? After all, it was not so long ago that they had made wild and exuberant love. But now there was Paul.

She tried to observe Paul surreptitiously as he discussed the various points with Richard. This guy was smart, persistent and well-informed. He'd done his homework, that was plain. Yet his manner was not bullying or bombastic. He seemed to care about the future of Weatherby's. And he cared about her, she was sure. But – excitement? Just what did she want from a man? Paul caught her eye and smiled; the widest, kindest, most inviting smile she could ever remember receiving. Its effect was overwhelming. Her heart danced with pleasure.

"There is some other news." The others looked at her with lively eagerness. "Your wedding won't be the only one. Paul and I are getting married – if he still wants me."

Julie's exclamations of joy were only superseded by Paul's astonishment. Richard just beamed through a mouthful of rice.

"It looks as though Paul is as surprised as we are," he said eventually.

Paul suddenly looked abashed. "Well, I am. I wasn't sure she'd have me. She's certainly made me wait for the answer."

"What did Irene say?"

"Erm, I haven't told her yet. But she did say that I wasn't to let Paul come to the house again. Would you believe, she wants me to marry George Quirke. Threatened to disinherit me if I thwarted her plans to persuade him to invest in the business."

Paul's eyebrows shot up at the news, but Richard looked thunderous.

"I hope you never agreed to that!"

"Don't worry darling – that would mean we get Kimberley's share of the money as well!"

Even Richard was taken aback at this swift assessment of the financial implications. "Forget it. Irene can't touch Dad's money in trust. And all she's got is debts as far as I can judge. Inheriting those won't get us very far. I'm surprised you signed over your rights when she mortgaged Prospect Hall, Kim."

"What rights? I never signed anything."

Richard was puzzled. "When she first raised money on the house, the bank insisted that all the adults living there gave written permission for the debt. I had to. Bob didn't because he had the flat in London and Irene said he lived there permanently. But you must have signed the waiver or she couldn't have got the money."

Kimberley's body froze despite the heat from her lamb madras curry. "I never signed anything!"

"Are you sure? I saw the form with a signature on it."

"Quite, quite sure. I didn't even realise she had mortgaged the house until she told me last weekend when she was making the case for me marrying George Quirke. The bitch! I even felt quite sorry for her – apart from the George matter, that is. So she must have forged my signature! That is unbelievable. And she's trying to control my social life and stop me having any contact with Paul, for example. She must be the wickedest stepmother since Cinderella!" Kimberley felt sick with anger. "That's it! I've had enough. I'm going to go home and have it out with her. I don't care what she does.

If she throws me out, so be it. I'll have no job, no income and, when she knows about Paul and me, no home either."

"She wouldn't turn you out, would she? She's your mother," said Paul, horrified at this turn of events.

Richard cut in. "You don't know Irene. She doesn't think like normal people. She possesses that deep cruelty that has a total lack of imagination. She's like Stalin without his humanity and charm."

"And she could make staying there pretty unpleasant. Where would I go? I have no money – except a growing overdraft." Her eyes circled the table helplessly, ending with a beseeching look at Paul.

"There's an easy solution. Before you say anything about the forgery, just promise to marry this other fellow. Then you can say whatever you like. She won't dare upset you, let alone tell you to go. You'll be too precious to her. Without you, she wouldn't get the money she wants."

There was silence as each considered the plan. Richard was the first to speak. "That's brilliant! Paul's right. It will be like a combination of toothpaste and deodorant, giving you total protection. You'll be able to lord it over her."

Kimberley was having difficulty in believing Paul had made such an awful suggestion. A wry smile began to displace the horror of it. "Won't that be bigamy?"

"Yes, very big o' you," quipped Julie. She was in fine form today.

"You don't have to go ahead with it. Just say you've changed your mind but you want a couple of months to get used to the idea. And get to know the man better."

"I think I know him quite well enough. God! What a load of unpleasant diseases I could be exposed to."

"And you could demand some cash to prepare for the wedding, as well," offered Julie. "If there is any left, you might as well get some of it."

Kimberley was thinking hard as she cleared her plate. "I'm not sure she'd believe me."

Richard laughed. "Every female I've ever known could act the pants off Meryl Streep. Just think of the satisfaction of taming the proverbial shrew."

"She'd be as pleasant as a king cobra. Defanged, of course," said Paul, adding to the metaphors.

"But she's bound to tell George and how will I avoid him?"

"Hurry up the completion of my house then you can live there. He won't be able to find you – at least for a few weeks."

Kimberley considered the situation. "I would then possess all the power, wouldn't I?" There was no triumph in her voice, no glee, no satisfaction. "And I could control the business." She said it with a cold calm. "It still doesn't sort out my future, though." Then her telephone rang again. This time she leapt up to go outside; the caller ID showed it was Lisa.

"Lisa! I'm so glad you've rung. How are you?"

"Give her my love," called Julie, as she hassled Richard to finish his meal and leave with her so she could return to her unruly thirteen-year-olds. Kimberley nodded abstractedly.

Her friend's voice was faint and hesitant. "I'm okay. I can't talk long. I'm at work."

"Yes, I heard. George Quirke made sure you got the job at the hospital. I'm so pleased for you. How's the nursing going? Is it as good as you expected?"

A pause. "Kim, are you sitting down?"

"No. I'm outside the Curry Palace where we're having lunch – Richard, Julie, Paul and me. Why?"

Another pause.

"Kim, there's something I've got to tell you. I'm working with the outpatients' records here. And I saw that today, a Frederick Galbraith was due back to check on his burns. He also has a broken ankle."

"Oh, I was wondering how he was getting on. No one's heard anything from him here."

Yet another pause. A longer one. "He came in this morning, so I made an excuse to go to the department to get a look at him."

"Yes – so?"

There was a strange, strangled sob. "Kim, it isn't Freddie. It's Bob!"

Chapter 13

There are posh parts of London and even posher parts of London (where posher = very expensive indeed). Bob's one-bedroom flat was in Bloomsbury, a posh part, convenient for the university. "But don't go there," said Bob, "it's been broken into. Come to the new place in Sloane Street." Poshest of the posh.

Disbelieving it herself, Kimberly had not told anyone else about Lisa's shocking revelation. But later that evening she had tentatively asked Richard about his identification of the body.

"Do you think I can't recognise my own brother?" he replied, discomforted at the gruesome recollection. "He was very badly burnt about the head."

"So, er…all his hair was burnt?"

Richard shifted uncomfortably in his chair. "Yes, it was. And his face was horridly burnt. Red. Almost shiny with that dried ooze. Have you ever seen a burnt dead body, Kim? Well, you don't want to. Now leave it alone, will you?" he snapped.

Kimberley left a long pause before remarking quietly, "So he must have looked very like Freddie the Unsteady."

Richard pursed his lips in annoyance, got up and left the room to avoid any further conversation on the subject.

Now she stood at the extremely posh flat. The security arrangements were as impressive as the address. But the names listed on a panel inside the lobby included Galbraith, not Weatherby.

Bob was half-hidden by the open door when she got out of the lift. As she entered, she could see that he was standing awkwardly, leaning on a metal crutch. His head was shaven, and he had a straggly goatee beard. He looked astonishingly like Freddie but younger and thinner, almost gaunt. And furtive.

His welcoming hug, albeit with his only free arm, was affectionate and intense. Kimberley's response was full of relief, certainly, but with little genuine warmth. Deception, fraud, impersonation, extortion even, the catalogue of his dirty crimes stood in stark contrast to the sparkling ostentation of the prestigious accommodation. He showed her into a smart, under-illuminated room full of sophisticated beige and brown textures and a huge, offensively shiny black leather suite. She sat down on the sofa diffidently. He hobbled over to one of the chairs and manoeuvred himself into it. An open car magazine lay at its feet. His facial expression was not easy to interpret. For some moments their eyes studied the other.

"So, you've not told anyone? Not Mum?"

"Not yet. Not before I've spoken to you. I promised Lisa. First of all, I had to check that it wasn't a cruel hoax. But you sure as hell have some explaining to do."

She expected her brother to look sheepish when faced with this challenge. In the gloom, it was disturbing to see instead what looked like a smug cockiness. He heaved himself up, grabbed the metal crutch that rested against the side of his chair and shuffled off to prepare some coffee.

"Unless you want something stronger," he offered.

"No thanks. Coffee will be fine. Just start talking."

There were the various clicks and gurglings in the kitchen as he went through the elaborate procedure needed these days to produce the wonderfully rich, aromatic, satisfying nectar. Another few moments and he was manoeuvring back with two mugs on a small tray he could manage to hold with the crutch-free hand.

Bob began to recount the story. There was no way of telling whether the narrative she was hearing was the truth, but at least Bob's version did not contradict in any way the facts as she knew them.

She learnt that it was not unusual for Bob and Freddie to frequent the same nightclubs – as they had on the night of the fire. No, it almost certainly wasn't a bomb. There was a big flash and an explosion in a corner and some wall covering went up in flames. Then the inevitable stampede for the exits. Bob with a few others chose one nearer to the fire because there was less of a crush. The passageway ran past some back offices. "They must have been reorganising or something because there were loads of these plastic crates along the sides, so the girls had lots of trouble getting past in their tight skirts and high heels."

It all took time for folks to move along and they could hear the fire tenders arrive before they reached the outside. Then a girl grabbed hold of him. "She was quite hysterical, and I couldn't understand her at first." She wanted Bob to go back inside to help; Freddie the Unsteady had lived up to his name and fallen, then been trampled on. Though still conscious, he was badly burnt, but his biggest problem was that he was half out of his mind with drugs. "Away with the fairies, he was, had absolutely no bloody idea what was going on."

Bob was able to lift and carry him but with the extra burden, he could not avoid falling over some of the crates. That was when he broke his ankle, but the crack was not as loud as the sound of Freddie's head smacking into the concrete floor. When they eventually emerged, Freddie was unconscious and Bob was coughing his guts out from smoke inhalation. Some paramedics bundled them into the same ambulance. There was a break in the narrative while Bob became hesitant and uncharacteristically secretive. "What you don't know, Kim, is that my life has been hell, recently."

"Why?"

Bob drummed his fingers on the arm of the chair in which he was sitting. "Er, there have been difficulties –"

"*Difficulties?* What difficulties have you ever had to face in life? You have an adoring mother and enough money to throw at any problem to make it disappear. You can have what you want, the friends – and girls – you want, the easy life you seem to crave. You've never had to cram late the night before an exam you have no hope of passing, wait in the pouring rain for a bus, count the pennies at the end of each month like others do. You never even have to endure loneliness. So what exactly are these difficulties?"

"That's not important right now," he said at last.

"I think it very much is."

Bob gave a frisson of annoyance. "I'll tell you later," he conceded grudgingly. "But I needed some cash – desperately. I'm brassic. So in the ambulance, I searched for Freddie's wallet – he was bound to have a lot of cash on him and the state he was in he'd never miss it. You know, his face was like shiny pink satin." He paused. "But also, er, there are some nasty people out there, Kim. *Very* nasty. And I suddenly realised that my life would be a lot simpler if I just disappeared."

Kimberley had to struggle to keep the shock out of her voice. But she knew what was coming. "So what did you do?" she asked with ice in her voice.

"I took all his stuff, didn't I? And replaced it with mine. When I got to the hospital, I said I knew him and booked him in as Robert Weatherby. But I think he was dead by then."

Bob drank some coffee with a nonchalant gesture. Kimberley watched him with growing disgust.

"Once I'd shaved my head and grew the goatee – quite fetching, isn't it? – sorted out the flat and moved in here, it all became pretty easy. I just wasn't expecting Lisa to see me."

"But you must have realised that sooner or later someone would recognise you."

"Why would they? Freddie and I look very similar, and the age difference doesn't count for much. With my hair shaved off and this beard and a different style of dress, I can easily pass for him. I could go on living here in solitude – it's very peaceful." He looked around him with a self-satisfied air. "I'd be a brooding, tragic figure, isolated by secret sorrows in tranquil luxury. With, at the moment, a very inconvenient broken ankle. But it's getting better."

"But what about contact with the Galbraith family?"

"I don't need to – just go abroad for a few years. And didn't I help you by sending that text releasing the land? I bet Mum was pleased!"

His childlike glee astonished Kimberley. "Have you any idea how many crimes you've committed? What you've done can't be explained by any cause or values. Just simple selfishness, a relentless pursuit of self-exoneration. You have a fearsome ability not to see the consequences of your actions, let alone care about them. For a start, Lady Galbraith doesn't know her son is dead."

"Oh, her. So what?"

Bob swung gingerly out of his chair, placed the empty coffee mugs back on the tray and, crutch seized, still managed to stalk out into the kitchen with youthful grace. "You sound just like mum," he hissed. "Why did you come if all you wanted was to criticise me? You have no idea what I've been going through."

"And whose fault's that?"

A hostile silence. Kimberley realised, that her approach was not going to solve anything but she was at a loss what to do next. A ringing on her mobile phone solved the immediate problem.

"Hello. Oh, James! Yes, I'm fine. How nice of you to ring. No, sorry, I can't talk right now, I'm with a friend" – the word came out a little too deliberately but James seemed not to notice – "in London. No, I don't know just when I'll be back, but a day or two at most. Yes, I'd like to see you and have a talk." Kimberley was thinking about telling him that she was now engaged to be married, but James must have thought she was hinting about another wild night. She was about to explain that was not what she had in mind when, to her surprise, her response to his call went from flattering to tedious. He continued extending hints of undefined mutual pleasure to come. She was generally unmoved by flattery but this degree of favour did merit a greater level of attention than she was comfortable with. She rolled her eyes at Bob as he returned from the kitchen, pointing to the phone and mouthing "James".

After a few more minutes of frustration, she managed to ring off without getting into any sort of temper.

Bob sat down opposite her, thoughtfully. "Be careful, Kim, where James is concerned. I know he's a great guy and you like him a lot but…" Bob was obviously not up to speed with the latest news.

"I'm not involved with him if that's what you mean."

"Good. I'm not sure all his friends are as nice as he is, and I wonder sometimes if he's not mixed up in something a bit dodgy. He seems to have too many secrets."

Kimberley nodded in acceptance of his advice, even though the giver was hardly in a position to criticise anyone else for improper behaviour. The words 'pot' and 'kettle' sprang to mind. She returned to the immediate problem.

"What do you intend to do now? Surely you aren't going to continue this charade."

Bob's air of bravado reappeared. "And why shouldn't I?"

"The money's going to run out for one thing. Sooner or later."

"Don't try and scare me. The Galbraith coffers are humongously deep. And if I wait a few years, the old bag's gonna die, everything will be forgotten and I'll be heir to a fortune!"

Kimberley chose not to inform him that his share in the business was being sold and his position as heir apparent could be downgraded to heir presumptive.

"But you'll be found out. And Julie's spending your Weatherby inheritance." She explained her friend's arrangements consequent on his death and was perversely gratified that it gave him pause.

"I'm sure our Richard will help her," he said. "And I bet you'll be spending your extra share too, won't you?"

Kimberley stopped abruptly and took a deep breath. "Dear God! What do you think I am! You've reached bedrock. You care about nothing and nobody and you judge everyone to be the same as you. What have you got instead of a conscience?" Kimberley cast her eyes around the room, at the money on display. "You take whatever you want without ever thinking through the consequences of your actions. You feel entitled to everything and responsible to no one. You have no principles except those dictated by greed and personal convenience. Even Irene would have difficulty forgiving you all this."

At last, there was a break in her brother's callous indifference to others. "She thinks I'm dead?" he asked softly. Was there a slight air of remorse?

"Of course she does!"

Bob squirmed in the chair and for the first time, looked both guilty and embarrassed. "What did she say when she heard?" he asked timidly, as though he'd been caught, pilfering forbidden treats from the pantry. His eyes had emptied of scorn and now held a glimmer of contrition. Or was it vanity? "Was she very upset?"

"I don't know how you can ask that!" Kimberley spat out. "What do you think? Try putting yourself in her place for once instead of thinking only about yourself!"

Was there a trace of empathy in his manner? Of embarrassment? Like a midsummer shower, it quickly vanished, leaving not a trace. His eyes roamed the room restlessly. Some quality in them – of despair, of shame – pierced her anger.

"Irene needs to know you're alive. Of all people, it's your mother you must tell. Not me – it's something *you* should do. And then maybe you'll realise the depth of your cruel deception."

"*Should, should, should!* I'm tired of always being told what to do!"

"That's absolute rubbish. No one has ever told you what to do. You've always done exactly what you wanted – endorsed and even promoted by your mother. You're as disciplined as a jelly, always astonished when things didn't go your way. You know, when I was little, I admired you – envied you almost – your carefree ways, independent thinking. But now I abhor it. You think of no one but yourself. You're letting your own mother continue to believe that you've been burnt to death and another mother doesn't know her own son's dead. That's apart from the responsibility you owe Anna and Lisa, of course." She slipped that in slyly to see whether his reaction was any different, now they were face to face.

"Oh, they're just nice girls who don't know how to keep their legs together!"

Kimberley rose in exasperation and turned to leave. This was useless. She needed to think about what she ought to do now. As she started to move towards the door, Bob asked again: "How did Mum react when she was told?" He paused. "I want to tell her and confess, but – but – if you knew how messed up my life had become... And Freddie's is so clean and simple. No worries. No problems. I just can't pass it up, Kim."

"And *your* feelings trump those of everyone else."

She sat down again as her mobile phone rang again. This time the caller ID showed Paul and she hesitated a little while deciding whether to answer it. Abruptly she diverted it to voicemail promising herself she would ring him back later. His considered thoughtfulness would be invaluable but at the moment, she wanted some space to make sense of this awful situation. She looked across at a sulky Bob who was fingering his Smartphone. Or, rather Freddie's.

She wandered around the room, examining the furnishings, ornaments and general living debris. "This is a classy place. But for someone rich, you don't spend much on heating. Don't you want it a bit warmer, not being able to move around much?"

"There's something wrong with the boiler. I've told the agents. They're sending someone round to fix it."

She sat down wondering how she was going to play this. How could she engender an attitude in Bob that would prompt true remorse and a confession?

Her phone pinged, telling her a text had been received:

"I've followed Bob's advice at last and just hired a car from some local firm whose name I forget. Does this make me one of the family?"

She gave a faint smile and put the phone away. She did not feel like any light-hearted banter right now.

"I think I'll go for a walk. You will let me back in, won't you?" Kimberley got up and walked across to the door. As she began to turn the door handle, the bell rang.

Bob frowned then looked alarmed. "Who can that be? No one knows I'm here. And how did they get through security? Do me a favour and open it for me."

"Why me? Are you so afraid, you daren't open your own front door? I thought you said Freddie had no problems. Open it yourself."

Bob's face showed real fear and pleading. Kimberley opened the door and saw two men. They did not look as though they were on a Sunday school outing.

Chapter 14

The taller man wore a suit (if the word can be used for such an ill-fitting arrangement of clothes) and had greasy black hair tied back in a ponytail. The other guy was as near to a Neanderthal as Kimberley could imagine: shorter, stocky, coarsely featured with overhanging brows – and so-o-o bandy. You could park a couple of hippos between his legs.

Pony Tail leant forward and leered at her. "So *you're* Flavour of the Month!"

"What do you want?" Kimberley cut in, fearing something very bad.

He took her wrist tightly, pushing her back as they stepped inside and closed the door behind them.

"So, where's Freddie? He's expecting us."

Not waiting for her answer, they drew her into the living room. "Hello there! Tried to escape us, eh? Made it difficult to find you. Nice place you've got here. But we're clever – and we haven't forgotten you owe us some money."

Bob's expression had gone from blank to horror. "I don't know what you're talking about," he muttered – as if that would terminate the encounter!

"Short memory, eh?" Pony Tail turned and smirked at Bandy, who leapt forward, grabbed Bob's arm and pinioned it behind his back. Bob's face screwed up with pain.

"A guy who can afford this place isn't short of a bob or two. And you owe us quite a few bobs. The guv'ner muttered something about five thousand quid for services rendered – or goods supplied, should I say. And he doesn't like bad debts. So here we are."

"I don't have that kind of money and leave my cousin alone."

Kimberley was trying to extricate her arm, fearing she would be the next one in an arm lock.

"Cousin? Oh, I was mistaken. I thought she was a bit on the plain side for you. I've seen you with much better tarts. But that's even better. Even if *you* don't have the cash, *she* will." He turned his grin to Kimberley.

"Thanks, Bob," she thought. *"Just what I need right now, getting me involved with this deception."*

There was a silence while each party considered the next move.

Ponytail's phone rang. "Yes, guv, we found him. But he's not being very cooperative at the moment."

Kimberley was sure the speaker on the other end said, "*Merde!*" Couldn't be.

"Don't worry, Trev 'ere is persuading him right now. We'll report back later. You can let him go now, Trev. Let's see whether he's telling the truth. See what cash they have here. We need some bread from Fred – or else he's dead!" He laughed at his superb rhyme.

Bandy reluctantly freed Bob's arm and set about searching the place from top to bottom. This took some time.

Meanwhile, Pony Tail sat himself down in the other armchair and watched his prisoners. Bob's wallet was retrieved with glee from his jacket and then Bandy seized Kimberley's handbag, brushing off the protests.

"About eighty-seven pounds cash but lots of cards; a credit and a debit card from him and *three* cards from the *lady*." The last word with a sneer. "And here are two rather nice phones – I could do with a new one."

"Eighty-seven pounds. Hmm, that leaves four thousand nine hundred and thirteen pounds to go. Well, we can start with the cards. Where's the nearest cash machine?"

Bob remained silent.

"You won't be able to use them without the pin numbers," said Kimberley, stating the obvious.

"*We* won't be using them – *you* will." He grinned at Kimberley. "And Freddie's going to give you his pin numbers, aren't you, Freddie with the Readies?"

"No point, there's no money left in either of them."

"Well, we can check that out. I'm sure your cousin will have some."

"There's a daily limit, you won't be able to get much from each card anyway," said Kimberley.

"Aren't you the helpful one, little Miss Know-It-All? But it'll be a start, now, won't it? Come on, love, get your coat on. Trev 'ere will stay with Freddie till we get back. Now write down the numbers for her. We can wait as long as you like."

Bandy moved forward, picked up Bob's injured leg and raised it slowly till Bob winced with pain.

Kimberley looked across at a sulky Bob who was now gazing after his Smartphone. Or, rather, Freddie's.

"Get him a pen and paper, love. What's your name?" he enquired. Kimberley threw him as filthy a look as she could muster and obeyed.

Still giving the occasional whimper, Bob wrote down the number. Ponytail then escorted Kimberley to the door, gripping her upper arm tightly. "Still don't know the nearest ATM?" he called back to Bob.

"About fifty yards on the left," said Kimberley, realising that it was all going to happen. Trying to stop it would be emulating King Canute.

"You can show me, darling. I'll keep tight hold of your arm so neither of us gets lost. Let us in when we get back, Trev."

They met no one on the journey and, even so, Kimberley could not think how to alert anyone's attention without endangering herself or Bob further. And no one could notice the excessively close attachment between the two of them. So they arrived back without incident. Just a bored acquiescent nod from the guy on the security desk.

"£1,500! Not too shabby. And we can get the rest over the next few days. Meanwhile, we'll keep the £87 for the inconvenience you've caused us – and the cards. You won't be needing them – you're not going anywhere for a while. And you won't need your phones either. 'Ere, this is for you," tossing Bob's to Bandy, "but I don't need a new one. Mine's newer, anyway." He threw Kimberley's against the wall where it smashed. Then Bandy stamped on the pieces while both laughed with childish delight.

Ponytail went over to Bob. "You're causing us a shitload of trouble, Mr Galbraith." He stretched out Bob's good leg and stamped hard on the ankle. Bob yelped. "That's to remind you to be a good boy in future."

The guys left chuckling.

"Great! Abso-bloody-lutely great! You've certainly got rid of *your* problems by this ruse. Talk about out of the frying pan – it looks like you've jumped into the fire now. What are we going to do for God's sake? And how on earth did you know Freddie's PINs?" she queried quietly, suspicious that the conversation could be heard if the visitors were still lurking outside.

Between sobs, Bob explained. "I just went to the bank and told them I'd lost everything in the fire. They knew all about it, of course. They replaced everything very quickly, no problem. Freddie must be a highly valued customer."

"That's gonna change if you continue. Let's get out of here, fast!"

"What are we going to do about money?"

"We're alive, aren't we? Let's cross other bridges when we come to them." She went across and opened the front door. Leaning against the opposite wall and grinning broadly was Bandy. She quickly closed the door, indicating to Bob the unwelcome guard.

"Damn! How long's he going to stay there?"

"All night?" suggested Bob.

Kimberley closed the door and sat down again, shivering with both apprehension and chilliness. "The sooner you get that boiler mended, the better. Talking about mending things…"

Kate went to pick up the pieces of her broken phone. The case was nearly intact, but it was hopeless, no signal nor connection, "Do you have a landline?"

"No, who does these days?"

"No cash, no phones, and prisoners. You've excelled yourself this time."

Bob whimpered faintly, "That Trev really hurt me."

Kimberly exploded. "For fuck's sake! Don't you realise the state we're in? They won't just stop at another £3,500. They'll keep on and on taking money, and we can't even contact the banks to stop it." A long pause. "What do you think it's all about? Drugs?"

Bob nodded. "Probably cocaine. It's the current drug of choice for Freddie's set. Or maybe one of the new synthetic drugs. There are loads now. James was telling me about them – even I can't keep up with them all."

Kimberley thought of James for a moment. Doubtful that he could help. Then Paul – could he help them now? Then Richard. But there was no way of contacting them. She wandered over to the window and looked out.

"Could we somehow get a note down to a passer-by?"

"The windows don't open, it's all air-conditioned. To avoid pollution from traffic."

Another long pause. There was no noise from the passing traffic either.

"We're absolutely stuck, aren't we? Not even a television to pass the time. Do you have any food in the house?"

"Coffee and a few biscuits. I have takeaways delivered because I can't get out."

"That's it – we can get something delivered and they can alert the police! Oh, no, we can't because we don't have any phones."

Gloom settled over them once more.

"You know there are two worlds out there, Kim. A good world and a horrid one. Sometimes they cross over and then your life is in the hand of strangers."

"Those guys weren't exactly strangers. They'd dealt with you before. They knew you."

"Knew Freddie, you mean."

"Mmm. So you fooled them completely. The likeness is – was – astounding. Like you were brothers, but…" she paused and studied Bob intensely. "Oh, my God! That's it! You're half-brothers, aren't you? And that's why Lady Galbraith hates Irene so much. Both of you have Sir Philip as a father. The randy old sod!"

Bob reflected. "Does this make Mum a randy old bitch?"

Kimberley was stunned by this new realisation.

"And she's always made out that no one could match her impeccable standards of behaviour. The hypocrite! I wonder if Dad knew? I bet he did. He was sharp. But he always really seemed to love Irene. It was always a one-way relationship though." She looked across at Bob. "And you're like a cuckoo in the nest. Or, rather, a tapeworm, predatory and comfortable. Sucking the lifeblood of the family for your nefarious purposes. And now draining another family."

"But Freddie did too! I suppose we are similar," Bob conceded. "Not in a way I'd want."

"You've done damn little to change it."

Both sat pondering this new information for some time.

The doorbell rang. They stared at each other warily. The guys couldn't be asking for more money – they knew there was no more till the morning. When Kim opened the door, Bandy stood there behind a middle-aged man in a smart navy boiler suit, carrying a large toolbox.

"Boiler trouble ma'am? The agency sent me."

"Oh, yes, come on in." But Bandy closely followed him, leaving no chance for advising the situation and getting help.

"In the kitchen, mate." Bob waved his hand in the direction, then looked hopefully at Kimberley. She shrugged and followed them. The guy opened the boiler cover and started poking around, watched by Bandy who cast intermittent glances at Kimberley to ensure no contact could take place. She grimaced and strolled back into the living room. Ensuring her back was towards the kitchen, she picked up her handbag and sauntered across to the window. She took out her train ticket receipt and scribbled on the back:

WE ARE PRISONERS

THIS IS NOT A JOKE

GET POLICE

She folded it small enough to fit into her palm and wandered back to the kitchen. The guy was reassembling the boiler. "Just a pilot light problem," he advised. "Should be fine now. I've reset the timer to come on now."

"Thank you so much," said Kimberley as she accompanied him to the hallway with Bandy close by. Now, how to give him the note so he wouldn't open it where Bandy could see? She thrust out her hand and shook the man's vigorously after opening the door.

"Thank you again," she said, partially closing the door behind him and turning to Bandy so the man could hear her ask, "How long are you going to keep us here?" She needed to allow the boiler guy to read the note and leave with some corroborating detail.

Bandy slammed the door shut. "Till we get all the money, darling. The guv'nor will be angry otherwise."

"Who's the guv'nor?"

Bandy grinned and tapped the side of his nose. "That'd be telling, wouldn't it! And since you ask, yes, a cup of tea would be lovely."

"We've only got coffee."

"That'll do fine."

She returned to the kitchen, closely followed by her guard, put the kettle on – she didn't like the look of the Quooker tap. Neither was she inclined to risk Bandy seeing her mess up with the smart new all-singing-and-dancing coffee machine. She found a jar of posh instant and put a spoonful into each of three cups. Then poured the water.

"Milk and two sugars, please darling."

"No milk. We take ours black, and without sugar."

"That'll do," but he quickly grabbed the opened packet of bourbon biscuits on the worktop as he went back to the door and let himself out.

In a low tone, she told Bob about passing the note. His face brightened. "What a girl!" but the compliment was not appreciated, "But the police! What if they suspect anything or start asking questions?"

"And who else can get us out of here?"

Bob massaged his ankle thoughtfully. "I never thought that having money would be a curse. You just exchange one set of problems for another."

"And you don't even actually have all that money."

Bob looked at her quizzically.

"Firstly, Freddie's shares in Braithby Business Solutions are being bought by the Indian company so you won't have any future access to that source of cash. Also, Freddie's not the heir. Sir Philip had an older daughter."

"But she died, didn't she?"

"Yes, but she had a son."

Bob looked both intrigued and alarmed. "How do you know this? And where is he? No, that's absolute rubbish. You're making it up to scare me. His daughter just disappeared."

"What if an heir just appeared?"

"Don't be so fucking stupid! Shut up and think of a way to get us out of here instead of just fantasising."

Kimberley fell silent to let the information ferment in Bob's mind. "By the way, I don't know whether this is a coincidence, but I'm sure I heard their guv'nor say *'Merde!'* during the phone call with Pony Tail."

Bob started but didn't say anything. He sat thoughtful without saying a word. Then he rubbed his ankle again and whimpered softly. Kimberly gazed at him with contempt.

*****

It was nearly an hour before the doorbell rang again.

Bringing his cup back? But no, it was a not-very-convinced police officer. He looked too young to cross the road on his own.

"Any trouble, Miss?"

Kimberley looked for Bandy. "Did you see a man loitering about outside here?"

"Yes, but he left."

She breathed relief, picked up the cup Bandy had left by the door and dragged the policeman inside.

They explained the situation but it was clear there was considerable scepticism. He was eventually persuaded to

183

escort them to the local police station where again they told their story.

"And neither of us has any money, phones or cards. And the banks are shut now. Can we please make a phone call?"

Now there was the problem of remembering numbers – all were safely stored on the phones themselves. Kimberley could only remember that of Prospect Hall and the family business. No one answered at Prospect Hall but the night duty officer obligingly furnished numbers for Richard and, after a bit of rummaging, that for Paul as a customer. Richard's kept going to voicemail but Paul answered immediately.

"I've been robbed of my cash, cards and phone. Please, please help me."

There was a pause before a bewildered response. "Of course." Paul didn't waste time asking exactly what had happened and they agreed to meet at a local hotel. "Okay, I'll be there as soon as I can. If there are any flights this evening, I'll be there later tonight. If not, I'll see about a private plane."

"Oh, thank you, thank you," breathed Kimberley before passing the message to Bob and hanging up.

Chapter 15

Kimberley made a poor breakfast the next morning, with competing emotions of sympathy for the victims of the episode and an attempt at cheerful positiveness to drive through the chaos to achieve a resolution. When Paul joined her in the hotel's restaurant he was tight-lipped.

"Have a good night?" Ironically.

Kimberley grimaced.

Paul had arrived just after midnight – long after a sceptical police officer had taken all the details of their ordeal – and quickly recognised Bob. He had the wisdom not to enquire any further at the time. Firstly, he had booked all three into the hotel for the night. Then Kimberley borrowed his phone to try and cancel all the cards. This took some time with no readily available information on contact numbers. She guessed that another three lots of cash had already been taken from her accounts – her overdraft limit was generous – but consoled herself that at least most of the alleged debt would have been settled. She did not get much sleep as frantic worries about the immediate future interrupted her relief that the immediate danger was past. Now Paul needed some reward for his tact and patience. She chose to give a sanitised version, not from prurience but to save time and explain essentials before Bob made an appearance.

Paul seemed deeply unimpressed as Kimberley recounted events. "It seems as though most of the world's upsets are caused by young males in their late teens and early twenties."

Before the abridged history was complete Bob arrived at the table looking both sheepish and haggard. He was still hobbling on crutches but now with another injured foot besides the one in plaster.

Paul looked at him in disdain. "So what now?"

Kimberley shook her head in despair. "I suppose, first of all, we need to tell the mothers the truth."

"Why did you not tell the police?"

"They wouldn't have let us out, would they?" exclaimed Bob.

Paul nodded in reluctant agreement. "And for both the mothers, I think the truth would be better coming from Bob himself rather than the police."

Bob shot him a furious look. "That's a great idea! You're thinking just like Kimberley! Lady Galbraith is a pompous bigot. Why should I be the one to tell her?" But as soon as he said this he sank back in his chair, covering his face with his hands.

"I can't go back home, Kim."

"Oh, yes, you can. And you are."

"And return to what? Lady Galbraith's fury, the family's reputation in tatters and maybe a jail sentence? And mum... I just can't."

"You have little choice. Forget your problems for once – try showing some compassion for the two mothers. Family *matters*, Bob! And not just ours."

Paul harrumphed. "Irene's hardly a person to shower with compassion – like feeding a baby rabbit to a starving python."

Kimberley was not pleased with the comment – not from someone outside the family – even if she felt obliged to agree.

"I just can't go!" reiterated Bob.

Paul lent back and sipped his coffee. "So Bob goes back home, tells Irene and Lady Galbraith he's sorry, and everything's all right. Is that it?" The hotel's muted background noises filled the awkward silence.

"Do you have any better suggestion?" queried Kimberley defensively, "First of all I need to call Richard to explain the situation. Do you have his number on your phone, Paul? And, Bob, you're going! Let me find out the flight times. My car's still at Ronaldsway so we can go straight home. I just need to talk with Richard first."

*****

"Duck, Bob!" exclaimed Kimberley as they pulled into the drive at Prospect Hall. He gave a strangulated moan in the back but obediently lowered his head out of sight of the house windows.

A sombre Richard opened the door and nodded Kimberley inside to the living room where Irene sat.

"I've not said anything," he whispered.

Irene was on good form, radiating disapproval. "What's all this about, Kimberley? Think you can just take leave from this job as well just when you want? You've got a nerve, young lady. You know you've been fired, don't you?"

"Please sit back down and listen."

"Look, I've had just about all I can take recently. I don't want any of your silly excuses and fantasy justifications."

Kimberley glanced at Richard, sat down beside Irene and gently took her hands. "Bob's alive."

For a brief moment hope suffused Irene's face to be quickly followed by intense fury. "I knew it! You just want to torture me with your impossible ideas. Just get out of here and leave me alone." She had snatched her hands out of Kimberley's grasp and was hurrying out of the room.

"He's alive and he's here," Kimberley called after her.

Irene halted and turned back to her. A long pause. "Where?"

"In the car."

"I don't believe you! You're playing me for a fool. Having a cruel laugh at my expense. You always were jealous of your brother."

Now Kimberley got mad. "Hardly! With a different mother *and* a different father, he's not my brother, is he?"

For a moment Irene stood there frozen. Then, before anyone realised, she stepped forward, thrust out her hand and slapped Kimberley hard about the face.

Richard promptly stepped between them and grabbed hold of Irene's arms. Kimberly put her hand against her stinging face. She knew she shouldn't have said that but couldn't stop herself turning the knife further. A surge of vengeful pleasure.

"Now I understand why you went to Sir Philip's funeral. It was a *family* matter, wasn't it?"

Leaving Irene quivering with anger, she stalked to the front door and beckoned to the car's occupants. Paul leapt out to help Bob with his crutches. Seconds later, Irene rushed past holding out her arms. She embraced Bob frantically.

"Thank God!" she muttered hoarsely.

"I don't think he had much to do with it," stage-whispered Kimberley.

Then Irene turned and screamed at Paul, "You again! I might have known! Get him out of here! Just go!" She and Bob remained clutching each other and both dissolved into violent sobbing.

The other three exchanged fraught glances.

"I'll take Paul home, shall I? Will you be all right here with them?"

Richard nodded. "What about Lady Galbraith, though?"

Kimberley sighed wryly. "I'll go there a bit later when things here have calmed down a bit. She needs to know as soon as possible and Bob just cannot do it. He'd make things worse – worse than they already are." She gave Richard a fervent hug and left the torrid scene.

*****

Little was said on the journey. Although Kimberley was now able to talk freely, she shrank from voicing any opinions. Every so often she flashed a weak smile across at him, a smile which was meant to indicate that she was coping, if not very well. Both avoided any deep discussion of the issues that lay ahead.

After a while some conversation emerged. "When do you pick up the hire car?"

"Tomorrow. They wanted to check out my Indian credentials and I wasn't expecting to need it anyway. A late dash to the airport was not in my plans at that time."

"I cannot thank you enough for all your help. I don't know what we would have done without you." Kimberley gave him a sincerely grateful smile. "The police were not very helpful. And I desperately didn't want to explain more than I had to. Now the family's left with clearing up the mess."

"Lady Galbraith is my grandmother. I feel I ought to be involved here."

"Maybe not yet. I'm not sure two major shocks at the same time is a good idea. Let's leave it for a few days. Losing both a husband and a son within a matter of weeks is bad enough. Hard to know whether suddenly gaining a grandson would be a good or a bad thing. Let me get Irene settled first. We've still got to work out how we can get Bob to confess. And when. There'll be a load of criminal charges."

"Maybe even manslaughter?"

Kimberley shuddered. "No, of course not." There was a pause. "We've only got Bob's word for what happened. No, he's stupid and selfish, but he's not evil. And if convicted…"

Paul pursed his lips in a wry grin. "Yes that would be as welcome to Irene as a steak and kidney pie to a vegan."

*****

Kimberley got back to Prospect Hall long past sunset. The house appeared to be in darkness. Richard's car was not in the drive. Kimberley let herself in and realised it was a long time since she'd last eaten. She rummaged in the freezer and found a Boeuf Stroganoff ready meal. One of Irene's better efforts at coping without Anna.

"Good enough!" she decided. Irene must be managing okay these days. Before heating it she poured herself, most uncharacteristically, a large gin and tonic. Not much tonic. When she placed the meal on the table in front of her, she found that her appetite had capriciously diminished. She was reflecting on the time she had just spent with Paul. In his arms, not making love, just absorbing the comforting strength of his masculinity. Whatever was to happen, things would turn out okay. And their future? No opinion surfaced from either of them. She was still picking at her meal when Richard walked in, looking drained.

"I've just been to see Lady Galbraith."

Kimberly gasped. "I was planning to do that later."

Richard put his arm across her shoulder. "No, Kim, it's time for me to step up to the plate. You've shouldered it all so far. I'm the head of the family – not Irene – and it was something I felt I had to do."

"So how did it go?"

Richard sat down and rubbed his face. "Not good. Not good at all. She wasn't going to let me in at first. When I told her she just collapsed. I called a doctor and I stayed with her till he came. He just gave her some pills then I left. I think he was arranging a private nurse for her. Poor woman. She's entirely on her own. Doesn't seem to have any friends or family. What is it with rich old women? At least Irene has some friends. Well, acquaintances, maybe. And work colleagues. That woman has nothing."

Kimberley pushed her plate away. Should she tell Richard about Paul? No, not yet. Maybe Paul himself should do that.

191

"How's Irene? And Bob?" Richard asked.

"Don't know. Haven't been in long. I've not seen either of them. They must be in the study."

They walked along the hall, opened the door and switched on the light. Empty.

"Maybe they've gone upstairs. Wait here." Richard hurried upstairs to inspect both bedrooms but quickly returned.

"No sign of them. Let's check if the cars are in the garage. Hello, who's this?"

Kimberley followed his gaze and saw a familiar car pulling up. "It's James, Bob's friend. I'm trying to avoid him. Don't let him know I'm here."

"He's got a young lady with him. Long dark hair. Very attractive."

"That will be his sister, Diane." Kimberley had crouched down out of sight. She heard a gentle knock at the door. Why not ring the bell? She crept nearer the door to hear the conversation.

"Oh, hello. I'm James, a friend of Bob and this is my sister, Diane. I've been abroad so I've only just heard the news and I've come to say how very, very sorry I am. Do you have any details about the funeral?"

"No, not yet. We're still making the arrangements. Some legal matters…"

"Can you tell me more about how it happened? I've only seen the newspaper reports."

"Er, no, sorry, I'd rather not talk about it."

"Of course, I understand," There was a pause. "I don't suppose you know what's happened to Freddie Galbraith. I've tried getting in touch with him to see how he is and even been to the Manor a couple of times, but there's either no reply or no one will let me in. I understand he returned from his London flat."

"Oh, who told you that?"

Another pause. Then a girl's voice. "The cards indicated that he would suffer some rather bad luck so we just wanted to know how he was. But 'Light' conquers 'Darkness'. There is a reason for everything. Nothing happens by mere chance or a whim. Everything is part of life's karma. All will be well."

Kimberley put her hand over her mouth to prevent anyone from hearing her spluttering giggle. It seemed a lifetime since something had amused her so much. What on earth would somewhat-lacking-in-imagination Richard make of all this rubbish?

"Sorry, can't tell you anything. He must still be in hospital."

"We've tried all the London hospitals and the agents of the flat – we don't know where else to try, especially as his mother won't speak to us."

"Don't you think we have other things to worry about right now?" Kimberley could hear Richard's anger rising.

"Of course, so sorry. Thanks, anyway, and please do let us know about any funeral when you can. Bye."

Kimberley heard the door slam followed by the car doors shutting noisily, the engine starting and the car leaving.

Richard came back in snorting with disgust. "Don't worry, Kim, they didn't ask about you. Just as well, I wouldn't trust that pair further than I could throw them."

Swallowing her irritation at not being mentioned, she enquired the reason for his mistrustfulness. But there was no specific reason. "Just something in their manner. And quoting predictions from 'the cards' didn't impress me either. Who does she think she is – Mystic Meg?"

"No, but maybe Gypsy Gladys. But she's right, though, isn't she? It's Freddie who copped it."

Richard gave her a disparaging glare.

*****

Nothing of significance happened over the next two days. Kimberley picked up the domestic duties, especially the ponies and dogs – which seemed to be fully recovered, from their alarming night-time assault. Richard spent long hours at work, researching the history of the firm's financial difficulties. Nothing was seen of Bob and only glimpses of Irene as she flitted in and out of the house in winter clothing at odd hours, not even stopping for a drink.

Immediately after lunch on the third day, it was Paul who rang the bell. Kimberley had been sending all her calls – including his – to voicemail. Texts were brief and consoling, hoping she was well. She couldn't face either explaining the situation anew or enduring well-meant but excruciating sympathy for Bob's supposed death. She opened the door to a Paul who looked downcast and puzzled.

"Are you okay?"

Kim smiled sheepishly. "Yes, thanks. I'm sorry I've not been answering my phone. I just wanted some time to myself to sort things out and recover. But I did read your texts – thank you for your concern. Do come in." Her voice sounded strangely formal but she reached out to him as he entered and felt her body melt in a long embrace. His warmth, kindness and the shared knowledge between them of the situation was healing. Then the tears started to come, streaming down her face. She laid her head against him and closed her eyes tightly, shutting out the horrible, chaotic world. As her sobs subsided, her breath caught in her throat. She felt vulnerable with him, desperately needing the comfort he could give her. Then the practical in her took over.

"Have you had lunch?"

"Sort of. But a cup of tea would be good."

Kimberley smiled happily (much to her surprise – the first for some time) and led him to the kitchen where he sat at the large table and thoughtfully watched her make the preparations.

"Let's assume you're coping well, you certainly look better than when I last saw you. What about the rest of the family? How's Bob?"

Kimberley paused momentarily. "We don't know. Richard and I haven't seen him since when we all got here. Let me just quickly check if he's in his room."

She dashed out and returned speedily. "No, he's not, but Richard and I didn't think so because there have been no sounds or other evidence. Maybe he's in hospital."

She passed over his cup.

"No, he's not. I checked," A pause. "How's Irene?"

Kimberley grimaced. "Hardly see her, but she doesn't look good. No news there either. Let's change the subject. What have you been doing, then?"

Richard fortuitously walked into the kitchen just then for a coffee and was in time to hear Paul say: "I went to see Lady Galbraith."

The siblings stared at him in astonishment. "The day before yesterday. A nurse opened the door and wasn't going to let me in. I explained it was about the family – important family matters. I could hear Lady Galbraith calling, 'Who is it?' so I said, loudly, 'It's about your daughter. I'm from India, and I have some news.' So I was let in and gradually worked my way round to the real reason for the visit. But first I offered condolences, etc. She sat stony-faced throughout and stared at me with dark piercing eyes. Then I said that I'd only seen Freddie once – at the funeral – and could understand why his loss was so great.

"'You understand nothing at all,' she snapped but she didn't throw me out so I persisted. Another mother who, despite appearances, has no illusions about her son." The remark was not lost on his listeners. "I reminded her that Suzanne had tried to get in touch and had written many times but never had a reply. She still didn't say anything even though we're sure she blocked all the letters to Sir Philip – or the solicitor did. And probably destroyed some of them. Then I told her that Suzanne had married an Indian man from a well-to-do family and had a child. She eventually died in a riding accident ten years ago.

"At this, she showed consternation and disbelief – probably thinking of the inheritance. She asked how I knew all this and where the proof was. I explained that all the documents and legal papers were safe in India. With solicitors."

Kimberley noticed that Richard was sitting up straight and looked very alert.

'Rubbish!' she exclaimed contemptuously. "Probably all fake!" Then she remained quiet and thoughtful for some time.

I didn't disturb her – she had a great deal to think about. Then she suddenly looked up at me and said, 'How do you know all this? Is this child – if it exists – trying to claim some money?'

"I didn't say anything, but couldn't help smiling a bit. At first she looked horror-struck, turned away from me and stood up. The nurse who had been watching us from just outside the doorway hurried over to help her and suggested I should leave before upsetting her more. But Lady Galbraith insisted I should stay then turned to me and said levelly, 'It's you, isn't it? I know because as soon as you walked in this room, I thought for a moment it was Philip, young and when I first knew him. The same height, shape, and that striding gait he had. It's you. You're Suzanne's child.'"

"Hang on a minute!" exclaimed Richard, leaping up from his chair. "Are you saying that Sir Philip is your grandfather?" Kimberley had never seen him so animated. "Did you know this, Kim?"

She nodded, a bit warily.

"Since when?"

"Perhaps a month. Not sure."

A cynical sneer flooded his face. "You don't waste any time, do you?"

Kimberley rose immediately to the insult but saw that Paul was waving his hand to calm things down. "Forget it, Kim. Not everyone thinks like you do, Richard. Let's leave it at that for now. And if you'll let me continue…"

Richard nodded gruffly and resumed his seat.

"Lady Galbraith didn't cry but seemed very emotional. Neither of us moved or said anything for some time. I asked if she wanted me to go. She said no, but I could see she was very tired and upset. So I suggested I call the next day – yesterday – and she agreed.

"When I saw her the next time, she was composed and formal but full of questions. Mostly about her daughter's life. We talked for over an hour till she was visibly exhausted and she invited me to have tea with her today. So I thought I'd better call in here first and let you know because sooner or later, she's going to start asking more questions, a lot of questions, especially about Bob."

Kimberley sat soberly, but Richard was fiddling agitatedly with his cup. A car was heard pulling up outside. Richard got up quickly to go and open the door. They guessed it was Irene. Voices could be heard, mostly his, but not the words. However, when Irene shrieked, both went out into the hall. They saw Richard holding Irene's arms, and he had either shaken her violently or was about to.

"Stop it, you're hurting me!"

"Where's Bob?"

"Safe."

"*Where?* He's a wanted criminal! Concealing his whereabouts is also a criminal offence! Or hasn't that occurred to you?"

Irene screwed up her face and a solitary tear escaped. After a few moments, she said, "Come with me."

Kimberley and Paul followed them out of the house and into the cars. "If we're to bring him back, we'll need two cars," observed Paul as he followed with Kimberley.

*****

There was a convenient lay-by opposite the field in which lay St Trinian's, a small, old, ruined church.

"What's this place?"

Kimberley shook her head. "I'll tell you about it later. Let's see what's going on first."

They all followed Irene through the gate from the road and across the long, tussocky grass, still damp from the overnight dew. The chain locking the side entrance to the little chapel had been cut and the padlock on it hung down uselessly. Someone did not want visitors. As they entered the roofless stone building, they could see Bob lying at one end, sprawled on some wide stone slabs where the altar must have been. He appeared to be unconscious. It looked as though a week's neglect had taken its toll on him. Around him lay a tarpaulin, a wet sleeping bag and the detritus of empty bottles and food packets. Kimberley was sure there was a faint fetid odour.

"What the hell were you doing leaving him here like this?" demanded an angry Richard.

"I wanted to punish him." Barely audible.

Richard stepped up to the inert form, bent down and said softly, "Bob, it's Richard."

Bob opened his eyes in alarm and struggled to reach the metal crutches that lay nearby.

"Don't worry, it's okay. We're here to help you. Just lie back."

Bob sank back on to the altar with a soft groan, shivered and his eyes glazed over.

Paul now stepped forward and eased up the legs of Bob's jeans. The plaster on one foot was chipped and sodden but otherwise intact. The other foot was swollen, a livid purple with discharging blisters and black patches. "Gangrene?" he muttered. Then he gently pushed Richard to one side and bent down over Bob.

"Let's get you to the hospital," he said softly and gently picked Bob up in his arms, as carefully as you would with a baby. He stood cradling a weak, whimpering boy.

"This man is sublime," thought Kimberley.

Richard put his arm round Irene while Kimberley gathered up the crutches and as much of the other stuff as she could carry. Then they followed Paul in a solemn procession back to the cars.

Chapter 16

It wasn't a very cheerful meal. The usual seasonal flush of goodwill had faltered. No one needed reminding that it would be their last Christmas in this house. And each had their own private concerns.

Bob's were undoubtedly the most momentous. They hadn't been able to save his foot and he was trying to get used to a new prosthetic appendage. The other foot was still encased in plaster, strengthened by an internal steel rod that was going to need surgical removal.

A more worrying cloud hanging over him was that of criminal charges, both in his favour and the more serious ones against him. Everything was waiting for the inquest. Despite lengthy, reassuring discussions with his lawyers, he was frightened. *"Hardly surprising,"* thought Kimberley whom he kept appraised of such matters. At her prompting he even sent a grovelling apology to Lisa, which she ignored, having terminated the offending item.

These days Richard seemed quite lost without Julie. "She thought she ought to spend her last Christmas as a singleton with her family," he explained. But his eyes said that her parents now had misgivings about her marrying into a criminal's family. Details about Bob's nefarious activities had leaked out despite the Weatherby's best efforts at secrecy.

Richard had now fully taken over running the business and was trying to sell it but the Indian car company had pulled out of any deal. Maybe they too did not want to associate with a family whose members had questionable activities. Irene seldom went into the office now. "And don't you dare try and reinstate that Kelly fellow!" she had admonished Richard.

"I didn't say anything – just nodded," he told Kimberley. "But he starts back at work in the New Year. Yes, he can be an awkward bugger but he knows what he's doing and the other guys like working for him. Irene will never see him; she doesn't go down to the workshop. Even when she did, there was always trouble."

"Do you think he was the intruder that night, who doped the dogs?"

"And knocked you out," as if she needed reminding. "I asked him that when he came into the office to discuss coming back. His face went the bristly pink of a prize pig and looked very uncomfortable but had the nerve to ask me what I was talking about. I didn't bother to pursue it. I'm certain it was him – or one of his mates. I'm just puzzled why he didn't take anything. Why did he do it?"

"To give us a scare? And then lost his nerve?"

Irene was a shadow of her former self. Apart from the occasional visits to the office, she mostly stayed in her study at home or her bedroom. Sometimes not even coming to meals. She was becoming increasingly forgetful and her concentration lapsed easily, though the children avoided any discussion of their present concerns. It seemed that a failing business, mounting debt, an icy heart and an empty bed had taken their toll of a fine intelligence. Still physically healthy, her mental health was now a source of concern. Privately the children did not doubt that the next step was some kind of sheltered accommodation. No doubt George Quirke could help here.

Housing was also a concern of the other three at the table. Prospect Hall was to be put on the market in the New Year. After all debts were settled, it was unlikely there would be enough equity for Irene to buy a house, but at least any rent would be funded for some time.

Richard and Julie were planning to buy a house anyway. Any timing issues could be solved if Richard moved into her flat. Presumably, Julie's family would hardly object to that. Access was a whole lot easier now the Town Commissioners had painted out the yellow lines, claiming they knew nothing about them. Julie had her doubts but Kimberley was careful not to suggest a culprit near home.

Bob, well, he'd been warned by his lawyer that his accommodation would for some time be at His Majesty's expense.

Which left Kimberley. The solution for the immediate future was blindingly obvious but she resisted thinking about it. It wasn't just her decision anyway. Would she and Paul be living here or in India? Paul's work would surely be the main deciding factor. And what about her work? She may not need the money but she hated the idea of being a kept woman. She'd fought against that for most of her young life.

*****

Paul had arranged to take Lady Galbraith out to a hotel for Christmas lunch so it was nearly dark when he arrived.

"So how did it go?"

"Surprisingly well. The meal was delicious, and she was very pleasant company."

"Oh." Kimberley was strangely disappointed. She had rather hoped that his Christmas meal was as dismal as hers, especially when consorting with the enemy. "So what did you talk about?"

"Lots – mostly about Freddie to start with – she's dreading the funeral. Then she talked about the history of the business. Sir Philip and your father seemed to have been great friends. What a shame there is such animosity between the two families now."

"There are reasons," muttered Kimberley.

Paul raised his eyebrows questioningly but didn't pursue it. "We also discussed the purchase of the company by – er – the Indian one."

"Yours." Paul nodded. "Did you never make the connection?"

"No, it was our London office that suggested the acquisition. Being listed, it was common knowledge they were struggling so the board just okayed it. When Sir Philip died – one of the founders and a major shareholder – it seemed a sensible move. I had no idea that it was based in the Isle of Man. I couldn't resist coming to investigate when I did find out. And guess who I met!"

"So we owe it all to Bob." Kimberley fell silent. "He's got himself a hell of a future now. How do you feel about him now?"

"I still like the guy, but you cannot excuse what he's done. The vast majority of offenders are fully mindful of the consequences and moral implications of their actions. They just choose to ignore it. Prison will give him plenty of thinking time. We must give him every support to get through it."

They were in the lounge sitting side by side on one of the sofas, Kimberley nestling blissfully by his side. She thought back to their first meeting and chuckled at the memory. "You know, when I met you at the airport you were *so-o-o* miserable. You just stared outside the car and when Bob and I saluted the Little People at Santon Bridge, you were crushingly dismissive of us natives!"

Paul lay back and smiled. "I remember being amazed seeing palm trees and wild fuchsia bushes – a fantasy countryside. You know, Lady Galbraith is just as fixated by the island's folklore as you. She even mentioned St Trinian's Church and told me the story about the Buggane; how he tore off the roof three times in revenge and no one's bothered to try and replace it again. Good move. If at first you don't succeed, give up. It works for parachutists. But I'm still puzzled why Irene left Bob there. There was no shelter. Out in all weathers. Was she trying to finish him off with pneumonia?"

"I suspect it was a kind of punishment for disgracing the family. I bet she gave him several intense earwiggings!" Kimberley sighed. "Like Irene, Lady Galbraith must be facing a very lonely future now. Not that Freddie could have been much comfort. Of course, George Quirke could try and woo her." Kimberley shuddered at his memory and snuggled closer.

"But she did mention something important, Kim. She wants me to inherit the house."

Kimberley sat up abruptly. "What did you say?"

"I explained that that could be problematic as I'm getting married." He paused.

"And...?"

"She asked for the details, obviously thinking it was to an Indian girl."

"You told her it was me?"

"Of course."

"How did she react?"

"She went very quiet at first then spat out, 'The spawn of that bitch!'"

Paul hugged Kimberley as she shrank back at the bitterness. "Then she thought about it and added that you weren't so bad – my own opinion exactly! But I can see that managing those two at the wedding looks like fun! So," – looking down at Kimberley and smiling – "do you fancy being Lady of the Manor?"

She gazed back into his eyes – warm, intelligent, playful. "Sort of *Mi casa es su casa!* But where would Lady Galbraith live? Or do we call her grandma?"

Paul laughed. "We could discuss all that. The house is big enough to carve out an annexe, or even build a new cottage in the grounds. There's plenty of room."

"Hmm. I'll have to think about it. But the prospect of running the whole estate does appeal." She mulled over the idea. "But wouldn't you need to stay in India quite a bit?"

"We'll have to work that out. But I do like it here."

He leant down and kissed her. A wave of liquid pleasure ran through her. They couldn't make love right now. Not here.

But the prospect beckoned to her and her body started to anticipate it. She pushed away all thoughts of the past. John had been waste of time and effort, James an exciting but flawed distraction. This guy was real, successful, strong, but kind, promising all she had ever wanted. Bliss!

"Do you have anything special you need to do over the next week? Or two?"

"No – just get to know my new grandmother, I suppose."

"So we'll be able to spend a lot of time together?" The hours stretched out enticingly.

"If you insist. Let's be grateful that we're not any of those poor folks who have to work over the holiday."

"Like Lisa," thought Kimberley.

"Like the police," said Paul. "Though they'll be extra busy just now. Did you hear they've just made their biggest ever haul of heroin and cocaine? They reckon it came in overland from Turkey via Holland. Freddie must have been a good customer. They've arrested a guy in Douglas, only a young guy, it seems. Dreadful business. They think he was the top importer and distributor for the whole of the UK. It works like a pyramid with multiple dealers working the clubs and bars – they're the ones who usually get arrested, but – what's wrong Kim?"

He looked down at her with concern and clasped her hands in his.

"Oh, nothing," she said softly but with great certainty. She smiled back up at him. It was all in the past now. No one was going to spoil her future.